CASTLE TWILIGHT
AND OTHER STORIES

Colin Thompson

Illustrations by the author

Hodder
Children's
Books

A division of Hodder Headline plc

A Caatalogue record for this book is
available from the British Library

ISBN 0340 64850 3

Typeset by Hewer Text Composition Services, Edinburgh
Printed and bound in Great Britain by
Mackays, Chatham, Kent

Hodder Children's Books
A Division of Hodder Headline plc
338 Euston Road
London NW1 3BH

CONTENTS

For Anne

CASTLE TWILIGHT

Hidden between cold black mountains deep in the heart of one of those dark forgotten countries in Eastern Europe, was an ancient castle. For over six hundred years it had stood brooding at the end of the valley, crouching like a vulture over a small village. Its grey walls and turrets cast their long shadows over the houses, throwing them into perpetual darkness. Those who lived nearest the castle walls never saw the light of day. They spent their whole lives by weak candlelight, feeling their way through damp corridors where tired bats slept among ancient rafters and soft hairless things slithered through the shadows.

Like all true castles, Castle Twilight had a king and queen. Thin and dark and fond of staring into his own armpits, King Marmite the Ninety-Eighth, descended from the Ancient House of Florian, could trace his family back into the swamps before evolution. With his heavy black eyebrows, and breath that could strip paint, he should have been the most terrifying ruler the town had ever

1

known. But appearances are often deceptive and none more so than King Marmite's. He tried to terrorise, he had had the best teachers, but he was afraid of spiders and scared of the dark. Small children only had to burst a paper bag for him to run crying into the bathroom.

Like every one of his ancestors before him, King Marmite was blessed with left-handedness. And it was a blessing indeed, for it is a well-known fact that left-handed people are the nicest, cleverest, most beautiful people in the whole world. It is also a fact that every day they are forced to put up with all sorts of deliberately right-handed things. Writing that goes across the page the wrong way, back to front clocks and a hundred other little things that right-handed people take for granted.

To counteract all this unfairness everything throughout the castle was set round the right way, or rather round the left way. The scissors were specially designed to really hurt anyone right-handed as soon as they tried to use them. All the doors opened the proper way round and all the teacups and toilet rolls were left-handed.

Queen Anaglypta was as tall and thin as King Marmite was short and fat. When they stood side by side they looked like a bat and ball – except a bat had more curves than the queen. On her left knee she had a tattoo of a pair of lips so the king could kiss her without having to get a pile of boxes to stand on. Queen Anaglypta always wore a pair of thick woollen gloves, not because, as many people said, her hands were horribly disfigured by an encounter with a wild frog, but because every time she reached down to pat the king's head, she speared herself on his crown.

Like all good royal families, there was a prince and a beautiful princess. Considering how ridiculous the king and queen looked it was amazing how beautiful their children were. There were rumours that the prince and princess were not

4

their children at all, that they had been made out of plastic by Artery the Wizard. But apart from a strange attraction the two children had for washing up liquid bottles, no one could ever prove anything. Prince Bert The Fearless was the most handsome man in the country, with locks of golden hair and skin like velvet. He walked like an angel; young women fainted away with delight as he passed and washing up liquid bottles grew dizzy and toppled into the sink. Prince Bert was also incredibly, incredibly stupid. That was why he was fearless.

Princess Chocolate was even more beautiful than her brother. Her hair flowed behind her like radiant sunbeams and her skin made Prince Bert's look like the surface of the moon. Princess Chocolate was not incredibly stupid. By the age of ten she had been to three universities and had seven degrees in very complicated things. She was just about perfect, and everyone hated her – everyone except the old and evil Count Velcro who was determined to marry her. Whenever Princess Chocolate passed by, all the washing up liquid bottles in the kingdom blew bubbles.

The castle itself was, according to many, alive. No one knew when it had been built, certainly long before records were kept. It had just 'always been there', or 'always been here', depending on where you were standing. Rumours came and went but the most popular one was that the castle hadn't been built by humans at all, and that it wasn't even a castle.

'It came from out there,' people would say, pointing mysteriously up into the stars.

'It's a giant spaceship, far away from home,' said others.

'Why?' said Prince Bert.

'Why, what?' said the king.

'Why is . . . er why is,' said Prince Bert. 'Why is it Thursday?'

'One day,' people said. 'The whole castle will rise up into the sky and fly away.'

It never did, but there was no doubt that it was a strange place with strange marks on the walls that no one could decipher.

'And that proves it comes from another world,' everyone said.

'No it doesn't,' said Artery the Wizard. 'It just proves you're stupid.'

But no one would swear an oath to say it couldn't possibly be a spaceship and Prince Bert spent many happy hours crawling through the sewers with a torch, looking for the engines.

To outsiders the castle was like a fantasy. From a distance, seen through the mist, it seemed like a beautiful dream. Towers reached up into the clouds, shimmering pink in the gentle sunlight. Flocks of bright blue birds fluttered with scarlet butterflies and gentle music appeared inside your head. But it was all a trick of the eye, a magic trick conjured up by the Tourist Board's Witches to make outsiders come to the town. Close up, the castle wasn't so beautiful. Green stuff oozed out from between the stones. It trickled down the walls, formed a slick on the moat and crawled off across the brown grass, muttering to itself as it slid down the drains. The nearer you got to the castle the more menacing it became. The gentle music became dark and scary. Crows the size of huge birds leered down from the battlements, their massive beaks full of bright blue birds and scarlet butterflies, and one-eyed creatures in wet

8

sacks pulled at your sleeves, begging for dandruff. Even the flowers on either side of the path seemed to reach out to touch you, and you knew if they did you would come up with a terrible rash.

High on the tallest tower of the castle stood The Crystal Bridge. It was the most beautiful bridge in the history of the universe, and also the strangest and most evil. Because no living thing, not even an ant, had ever crossed it and come back to tell the tale.

Like the castle itself, no one knew when The Crystal Bridge had been built, it had simply always been there. Some said it had been there in the sky before the castle and that the castle had been built up to reach it. Most people, even those fools who laughed at the idea of life in outer space, agreed it could not have been built by human hands. It stood on the top of the tower and sparkled in the weak sunshine like a million diamonds. Some people believed it was actually carved from one enormous diamond. It vanished up into the sky, breaking up the light into a giant rainbow. No one knew where it went because the far end was shrouded in a permanent globe of mist.

A thousand rumours sprung up around The Crystal Bridge. One told of a small girl who had wandered across it only to return in the shape of four chickens called Brenda.

There were at least three groups of bridge worshippers who made wild fantastic predictions. One group said that some day a beautiful princess would come to lead them across into paradise; another that a big, red bus would appear out of the mist and save the world. Just to be on the safe side they built a magic ring of bus stops at the start of the bridge.

Some people believed that only a king or queen could walk safely onto the bridge but none had ever tried. At the slightest mention of it King Marmite always ran and hid in the toilet.

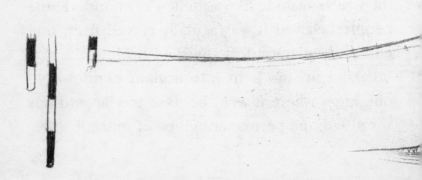

Castle Twilight had not always been a place of gloom and decay. A hundred and fifty years ago it had lived in sunshine and been the centre of the scientific world. Many great inventions were created there and it was the first building in the whole world to be lit by electricity, for it was there that the famous professor Dr Pelham Bulb invented electric light.

Weighing the invention in his hand King Marmite's great-grandfather had said the immortal words: 'It's very light, Bulb. What are you going to call it?'

'A photocopier?' suggested the inventor.

Ten years later Dr Bulb invented the light switch so they could turn off the light and went on to invent the electric sofa, a friendlier early version of the electric chair, electric sox and electric toffee.

To generate the electricity, tiny hydro-electric dams were built in all the gutters and because this meant the house had no light except when it was raining, huge windmills were built on the roof to pump water up from the lake beyond the town.

In those great days of scientific discovery, when a man could die of toothache at the age of fourteen, it was the king's dream to boldly go off into outer space to look for adventure, and a dentist. Night after night he toiled away over his drawings until at last he had invented the first coal-fired spaceship.

The problem was, he didn't know which bit of the sky to boldly go off into. There was only room on board for enough coal to travel one or two light years, so he had to be certain he knew exactly where he was going. This is why the Great Seven Man Double-Bass Intergalactic Telescope was built. Wrapped up in his thick woolly muffler the young king spent long clear winter nights closely scanning where no man had scanned before.

Unfortunately the king's dream was never fulfilled. No suitable planets were ever found to boldly zoom off to. He found fourteen planets in the farther reaches of space, where there were no signs of intelligent life, but he never found one single planet that had the coal he would need for the return journey. He died a disappointed man and the remains of his un-launched rocket stand on the roof to this day.

For the sake of his father's memory the new king carried on the search until one dawn he forgot to replace the five metre lens cap. The midsummer morning sun blazed into the telescope, shining straight into a bowl of petrol that the king had just put on the floor for his dragon's breakfast. The results were disastrous and it was eighty-three years before the door handle was cool enough for anyone to enter the observatory.

There were hundreds of rooms in the castle. No one knew exactly how many, but at one point twenty-seven estate agents were summoned to the castle and ordered to count them. For ten years they walked the corridors with their clipboards and pens until finally they all went insane. Of course, being estate agents, it was difficult to tell the difference but one by one they threw themselves off the tallest tower, or what they thought was the tallest tower, because they were never quite sure that there wasn't another tower they hadn't counted that was just a bit taller. After that, whenever anyone asked how many rooms there were, the king just said, 'more than ten,' in such a way that they never asked again.

Every room had its own story to tell and on midsummer's nights, when seven goats gathered in the town square at the same time as the planet Jupiter lay directly opposite Princess Chocolate's bedroom window, and a thunderstorm rained green frogs down all the chimneys, the rooms actually told their stories, and they told them all at once. The noise was deafening. Windows shattered, people buried their heads under mattresses, cats went bald, rivers boiled and all the witches smiled.

Castle Twilight was not a place you easily forgot. No matter how you tried. Once you had entered its walls, its memory was implanted in your brain forever.

THE MUSHROOMS OF THE MOON

The dungeons dark below the ground,
　　Shut off from sun and moon,
Are far from hope and far from sound,
　　An endless afternoon.

On walls of stone as wet as tears,
　　Drowned by ancient eyes,
You will meet your deepest fears,
　　And very old meat pies.

And here ten floors below the land,
　　In the devil's dark cocoon,
Where torches flicker in the hands,
　　Are the Mushrooms of the Moon.

The Mushrooms of the Moon

Just one bite is all it takes,
  To weave its awful spell,
You'll get the horrors and the shakes,
  Not only that, you'll smell.

And just like Alice you will change,
  But only here and there,
Bits of you will look quite strange,
  Or suddenly sprout hair.

Your legs might grow as large as trees,
  Your ears be hardly there,
Your eyes might move down to your knees,
  Or in your underwear.

So even if your appetite,
  Cries out – 'Please feed me soon',
Never, never take a bite,
  Of the Mushrooms of the Moon.

THE FRONT DOOR

The front door dates from 1523. Life was extremely awkward until it was built, as everyone had to climb in and out of the windows.

The gigantic doors are made of a strange alien wood from the dashboard of a huge spaceship that had been preserved in a peat bog since the Stone Age. The smallest inner door was carved from the headboard of a Roman emperor's bed. The rest of the bed had been used to make a very early form of airship, which was not a financial success. It was not until the wood was replaced with air that it actually flew.

To the left of the door is a small open container of penknives and a brass inscription inviting visitors to carve something in the door posts while they are waiting for the bell to be answered. On one famous occasion when the butler and all seventeen under-butlers were down in the deepest cellar hunting the elusive moon-mushroom, a particularly artistic visitor was kept waiting for so long that he managed to carve a detailed story of The Creation, three life-like bowls of fruit which included such exotic offerings as kumquats and prunes, and a scene from Snow White And The Seven Dwarves. By the time he was finally admitted he had got married and settled down with a small family. The final blow was that when he eventually managed to remember who he had come to see, they turned out firstly to have lived next door and secondly to have died seventeen weeks before.

Other carvings include a small ferret by King Haakon Knute the Fourteenth of Denmark and a minute replica of King Haakon Knute the Fourteenth gnawed by a remarkably talented ferret.

In the good old days as many as six hundred and fifty bottles of milk could be found on the doorstep each morning. But over the years this number has grown less and less. Today there are no more than a few pints of semi-skimmed and an occasional banana yoghurt.

There is no letter box.

Artery the Wizard

Two hundred and fifty years ago there were no wizards at Castle Twilight. The king and queen at that time had to rely on witches to do their spells for them. But witches were unreliable. If you got them on a bad morning they'd as soon turn you into a bag of porridge as make the sun shine.

'What we need is a wizard,' said the king.

'That's all very well,' said the queen. 'But where are we going to find the sort of money to get a wizard?'

'We don't need to,' said the king. 'We'll make one.'

'It's not a cake we're talking about here,' said the queen. 'It's a living breathing person.'

'I know that,' said the king. 'But I have a plan.'

'A plan said the queen. 'What plan?'

'Out of a magazine,' said the king. 'A plan with diagrams and a list of all the things you need.'

It was true. In the March 1747 issue of *Do-It-Thyself-Monthly* there was a full set of instructions on how to make a wizard. Of course it was only a toy wizard, a model like an action man, but the king hadn't bothered to read all the small print and thought he was going to make a real wizard. So he collected together:

749 wooden sticks

2 cheese rolls

A pair of red socks

Sticky tape (in 1747 sticky tape was made out of
woven grass and dog spit)

3 pints of beer

A three pin plug (the king had a lot of trouble
with that one because he couldn't understand
how you could make a plug out of three pins
that would stop the water running out of
the bath)

2 French-speaking goldfish

2300 miles of string

2 thimblefuls of antsick

A banana (in 1747 bananas were made out of
sticky tape)

A pinch of salt

4 Nails

A bald rat

17 Slugs

A bag of air from the North Pole

And a partridge in a pear tree.

'The pinch of salt was the hardest,' he said to the queen. 'I kept dropping it. Mind you the ants kept missing the thimble.'

The queen wished the telephone had been invented so she could ring for someone to come and take the king away.

It took him nine weeks to put all the bits together. The instructions were full of complicated words he didn't understand, like crease and attach. But at last he had finished and with very few bits left over. And what he had made looked like this:

'I think it's broken,' said the king. 'It's been sitting on the shelf for two weeks and hasn't done a single spell.'

'It's just a model,' said the queen. 'It's a dolly. It won't do anything.'

'Maybe it's sulking,' said the king.

'It's rubbish said the queen and when the king went off to the toilet she threw it on the fire.

And the fire threw it straight back at her. Suddenly its hair was smouldering and its eyes shone like burning coal. It grew so hot that the queen dropped it on the floor. For a second it seemed to crumple up and then it unfolded and kept unfolding until it was as tall as a man.

'Your majesty,' said the wizard, bowing to the queen. 'You have brought me to life and I shall forever be your servant.'

'Cool,' said the queen, which in 1747 didn't mean what it means today. In 1747 it meant 'you are on fire and if I were you I would get some cold water and put yourself out'.

When the king came back and saw what had happened he began the longest sulk in the whole history of sulking. He had spent weeks of loving care making his model and nothing had happened. The queen had thrown it on the fire and in a couple of seconds it had turned into a wizard. It wasn't fair. In the whole history of fair it was the unfairest thing that had ever happened. Even when the wizard went on to make jelly-babies appear out of thin air, and turned all the spinach into chocolate ice-cream, the king carried on sulking. The wizard gave him six birthdays in one month but the king *still* kept on sulking.

What made it worse was that everyone else thought the wizard was wonderful. He did nice kind happy spells that made everyone nice and kind and happy, except the king.

'Can't you just do a spell on *him?*' suggested the queen to the wizard.

'But I want him to love me for myself,' said the wizard, 'not just because I put a spell on him.'

'Great,' said the queen. 'Before all this started I had one idiot. Now I've got two.'

This made the wizard sulk too. He walked through puddles kicking the dirty water all over his trousers. He sat in the mud and stood in the rain and refused to eat sweets.

'I'm wetter than you are,' said the king as the two of them stood knee deep in the moat in a thunderstorm.

'No you're not,' said the wizard.

'I'm muddier than you are, too,' said the king.

'Aren't,' said the wizard.

'I'll hit you,' said the king.

'Well, I'll hit you back,' said the wizard.

'Well, my big brother's a policeman,' said the king.

'Not any more he isn't,' said the wizard waving his wand. 'He's a sausage sandwich.'

'What sort of sausage?' said the king.

'Chicken,' said the wizard.

'That's my favourite,' said the king.

'Mine too,' said the wizard.

'I'm cold,' said the king.

'Here,' said the wizard, and he made the rain stop and the sun shine and the king's clothes leap off him into a tumble-drier and back onto him again before he had time to be embarrassed.

After that the king and the wizard became best friends and spent hours making things together out of *Do-It-Thyself-Monthly,* including Creepeasy the Butler's grandfather and the Queen of England.

MEDDLER AND LEAKY

Castle Twilight dominated the whole town. Its windows looked out like empty eyes, black as the night, like the eyes of a blind man, but they saw everything. No one could ignore them. No matter where people were, even in the deepest cellar, they always felt they were being watched. And they were. High in the western turret, in a round windowless room two blind witches gazed into the souls of every living creature. From the richest man in town to the poorest rat in the deepest drains, Meddler and Leaky, the High Priestesses of The Ancient Order Of The Long Nose, spied on everyone. Whatever anyone did, the king and queen would know about it. At least that was the idea.

Meddler and Leaky were identical twins born in a drain on the damp side of town and they were the most important witches in the land. By the age of eighty-seven, an age when most witches have hardly left school, Meddler and Leaky were already the High Priestesses of The Ancient Order Of The Long Nose.

To be a High Priestess of The Ancient Order Of The Long Nose, a witch didn't need a particularly long nose, just a desperate desire to know every little piece of gossip there was to know. Meddler and Leaky were the two nosiest witches in the whole history of being nosey. It wasn't enough to know the colour of everyone's toilet paper, they had to know how many sheets every single person had used that day or they could hardly get to sleep at night. Not that they did sleep at night, for nighttime was the best time for peering into other people's business. They also had to be as blind as bats.

They saw everything but heard nothing. They saw people huddled over tables, buried deep in conversation, but they couldn't hear a word. They watched as people whispered secrets over garden walls but they never knew what the secrets were for they were both as deaf as posts.

'But if they're blind,' said one of the committee when Meddler and Leaky had applied for the job, 'how can they see everything?'

'They don't look with their eyes,' said someone else. 'It's all done with the mind.'

Which was true, except that if you were deaf,

like Meddler and Leaky, you couldn't hear what people were thinking. So they learnt to lip-read.

But they never got it quite right. For years the two witches managed to keep it secret, but when two-week-old babies kept getting arrested for shoplifting and a ninety-eight-year-old great-great-grandmother was reported to be marrying a chicken, Artery the Wizard began to realise something was wrong. It was he who paid their wages and he was furious.

'No chicken would marry anyone as old as that,' he said.

'Well, er,' muttered Meddler, 'that's what she said.'

'Absolutely,' said Leaky. 'Unless she said she was *marinating* a chicken.

'There's no such word as marinate,' said Meddler.

'Yes there is, stupid,' said Leaky. 'It's a place where you keep your yacht.'

'I haven't got a yacht, stupid yourself,' said Meddler.

'SHUT UP, SHUT UP,' screamed Artery. 'And what was all that rubbish about King Arthur and the Knights of the Brown Table? You had the whole town rushing round with tins of paint.'

Meddler and Leaky were pretty useless, but the trouble was there was no one else to do the job. When the howling storms of winter came raging up the valley, no one else could see through the snow and find the sheep. When the king lost the keys to his personal lavatory, no one else could see where he'd left them, though they did cut it a bit fine a few times.

'You're deaf, aren't you?' said Artery.

'What?' said Meddler.

'Who said that?' said Leaky.

'DEAF!' shouted Artery.

'There's no need to shout,' said Meddler. 'We're not deaf.'

'Half-past three,' said Leaky.

'Ah ha, caught you out,' said Artery.

'Caught a trout?' said Meddler. 'I like a nice bit of fish.'

'What bit?' said Leaky.

'The ears,' said Meddler. 'If you eat them you can hear in the dark.'

'That's carrots,' said Leaky.

'Carrots haven't got ears,' said Meddler.

'SHUT UP, SHUT UP,' screamed Artery again. 'You're driving me crazy.'

'Oh, I loved that film,' said Meddler.

'What?' said Artery.

'Driving Miss Daisy,' said Meddler. 'I thought it was a wonderful film.' Artery went into the corner and started banging his head against the wall.

'What's the matter with him?' said Leaky.

'I think he's trying to have a headache,' said

Meddler.

'I'd rather have a cup of tea,' said Leaky.

'And a biscuit,' said Meddler.

'Risk it?' said Leaky. 'Risk what?'

'Hold on, something's happening,' said Meddler, after Artery had gone.

'Of course it is,' said Leaky. 'Something's always happening.'

Meddler huddled over the crystal ball and muttered to herself. She spat on the ball and polished it with her cuff. Leaky peered over her shoulder.

'Shall I put the video recorder on?' she said. 'Is it something good?'

'It's that ghastly dog that keeps chasing carts,' said Meddler. 'He's doing something with that old chicken.'

'What, again?' said Leaky. 'That's boring, change the channel. Let's see where the old wizard's gone.'

'Yeah, maybe we can hassle him,' said Meddler.

A tiny room came into view in the crystal ball, cold grey walls running with damp, lit by a single weak light bulb, and there in the narrow space between them was Artery. He was huddled over a table with his back to them. The old wizard was bent almost double and his right arm was jerking up and down. And he was muttering to himself.

'You'll have to send your mind down to go round the other side of him and see what he's up to,' said Meddler.

'Alright,' said Leaky, 'but if I'm not back in five minutes, you'd better throw a bucket of cold water over me.

Of course, it was only Leaky's mind that went down into the wizard's room. Her body stayed where it was, leaning over her sister's shoulder, hardly breathing, staring hypnotised into the crystal ball. Meddler watched as the air in Artery's room shuddered. The old wizard could feel there was a presence and leant over further to try and hide what he was doing. His eyes darted round the room but Leaky's mind dodged out of their way as they passed her. There was a silent pop and the old witch was back inside herself again.

'Did you see what he was doing?' said Meddler.

'Yes, it was awful,' said Leaky.

'What, what was it? A terrible spell?' said Meddler.

'Worse than that,' said Leaky. 'I can hardly bring myself to say.'

'Force yourself,' said Meddler through gritted teeth, 'before I turn you into a pair of underpants.'

'He was colouring in with crayons,' said Leaky. 'A picture of fluffy bunnies.'

'Well, well, well,' smiled Meddler. 'I hope you took a photo.'

'Oh yes,' said Leaky. 'I dropped the film off at the chemists on my way back.'

'Excellent,' said Meddler. 'Nothing like a spot of blackmail to keep a wizard in his place.'

'Where did you get these?' said Artery, later, when they showed him the photos. He went as white as Creepeasy the Butler and all the veins stood out on his head like a road map.

'What did he say?' said Leaky.

'Do we want some cheese,' said Meddler.

'Why's he got a map of Timbuctoo on his forehead?' said Leaky.

'That's not a cockatoo. It's his veins,' said Meddler.

'He's vain?' said Leaky. 'You wouldn't think it by the way he dresses.'

Artery looked as though he was about to burst. He reached into his robes and pulled out a wand which he started waving in the air. He knew that no magic he could do would over-power the witches, but he was so angry he wasn't thinking straight. He shouted and screamed every awful spell he could think of. Suddenly, chickens appeared from nowhere, the table and chairs turned into three thousand pork sausages, the windows turned to stone, and where the door had been there was a pig's bottom sticking out of the wall.

'Temper, temper,' said Leaky.

'Oh that's clever,' said Meddler. 'We're stuck in the dark and the door's vanished.'

'You're two nasty evil disgusting old witches,' shouted a voice from across the room.

'Flattery,' said Leaky, 'will get you nowhere.'

'What do you want?' said the wizard.

Meddler reached into her apron pocket and pulled out a thick notebook. She handed it to the wizard. He sat down on the sausages and began to read. An hour later he was about halfway through.

'This is ridiculous,' he said. 'Do your laundry? There's no way you're getting this.'

'Well, we're open to negotiation,' said Leaky.

'OK, here's my offer. You can have nothing,' said the wizard.

The witches said nothing. They got up and looked down at the wizard, who was slowly sinking into the pile of sausages. Meddler made some magic hand movements behind her back and very slowly the sausages began to melt into each other. By the time Artery noticed, they had changed into a gigantic mouth and where the tongue should have been was where he was sitting. He tried to pull his wand out of his pocket but his arms were held tight. Slowly the huge mouth began to swallow him.

'Bye,' said Meddler, walking towards the door.

'See you,' said Leaky. 'Oh no, sorry, we won't.'

'Alright, alright,' cried the wizard. 'I give in. You win.'

'You twins,' said Leaky. 'We know we're twins.'

And at the end of the day everyone was happy. Artery the Wizard was happy because he no longer had two witches hassling him. The king and queen were happy because the wizard did wonderful magic for them. And Meddler and Leaky were happy because they were disgustingly rich, and were always dressed in well ironed cloaks and aprons.

HOUSE RULES

There were over fourteen thousand House Rules at Castle Twilight. Some had been written so long ago that the words had faded away and become impossible to read. Many of them referred to squeaky armour and the polishing of cannon balls. Here is the last recorded top twenty.

1. Bread and Butter Pudding shall not be consumed, cooked or even talked about.
2. No blunt scissors.
3. No jitterbugging or eccentric dancing (except on days containing a 'd').
4. All nasal hair to be trimmed before entering the premises.
5. Christmas not to be held more than twice a year.
6. No one below the rank of immortal to use the Executive Toilet (key under bucket).
7. No smoking or politics.
8. No ferrets to be thrown out of open windows.
9. No chewing gum or bogeys to be stuck under the edge of the table.

10. All wooden legs must be given three coats of gloss varnish and treated for woodworm once a week.
11. All dead bluebottles are the property of the king and may only be eaten if he has had enough.
12. All dischcloths must be properly wrung out.
13. Early closing March 25th.
14. Cling film only to be stretched across the toilet bowl after sunset.
15. Everyone under the age of fifty-five must play Tetris at least three times a day.
16. Toilet rolls to be hung face out from the wall.
17. All doors, spoons and labradors to be left-handed.
18. Anyone found leaving the bath dirty will be forced to lick it clean or face up to twenty-five years imprisonment. (Please state preference.)
19. No liquorice.
20. Left-handed people must be given double chocolate rations.

Other House Rules may be referred to in due course.

STRANGE FOOD

B ehind the castle, beyond the outer walls, lay
the moat. In its foul green waters, in the shade
of weeping willows, that had plenty to weep about,
lived the pukeworms. They were strange creatures
that had lived on earth for millions of years. While
other animals had evolved from tiny bugs into
horses and giraffes and humans, pukeworms had
evolved backwards, as if nature had got stuck in
reverse.

They had seen dinosaurs come and go, watched
the emergence of man, and through the millennia
had slowly sunk further and further down the chain
of life. Half-fish half-ferret, they had once stood
on two legs and played cricket with the alien
life-forms that had built Stonehenge. Now they
crawled through the centuries of mud and bones
that lay at the bottom of the moat, their scraggy
fur matted with twigs and deadmen's toenails. A
fluorescent slime on their skin made them glow
in the dark and their eyes shone like black pits of
despair.

King Marmite adored pukeworms. His favourite

waistcoat was made of their skins. His favourite
cufflinks were made of their eyeballs. His favourite
cuddly toy was made of their fur and his favourite
hobby was trying to train them to fetch a stick. He
loved everything about them but most of all he
loved them on toast.

A small tunnel from the castle kitchens led out into the moat and every dawn Toxic, the Royal Pukeworm Keeper, rowed out to catch one for the king's breakfast. Like his father before him and his grandfather before that, Toxic knew how to lure the creatures into his net. He polished a cricket ball with linseed oil until it shone like a ruby, put it into a funnel-shaped net and lowered it over the side of his boat. The smell of oil and red leather reached out into the water and, deep inside the pukeworms' ancient memories, something stirred, something from the days before time when their ancestors had stood in fields of grass and worn white trousers. It was a smell that no pukeworm could resist and they would swim blindly up into the net, and their destiny.

In the same way that no one but the Queen of England is allowed to eat swans, no one but the king was allowed to eat pukeworms.

'Well who would want to?' said the queen.

'You can, my beloved,' said the king. 'The queen is allowed to eat them too.'

'No, sweetheart,' said the queen. 'I'm sure she's not.'

'Can I have one?' said Prince Bert.

'No you certainly can't,' said the king. 'Not until you're the king.'

'Oh, but daddy,' said the prince, 'they look so delicious wriggling through the strawberry jam.'

'Shut up and eat your slugs,' said the king. 'And that's not strawberry jam.'

Sputum the Pukeworm Cook was driven half-mad trying to think of new ways to cook the king's breakfast. He had fried, boiled, roasted, grilled and microwaved the poor disgusting creatures in every sauce under the sun but still they tasted terrible. Or at least they smelled as if they tasted terrible, because not even the cook was allowed to taste them which made it very difficult for him to do his job properly. There was no way he could ever know if he had put too much pepper in the sauce or if it needed more salt or if the custard was lumpy enough. Over the years he had created many tempting delights for his majesty but although the king always said how wonderful every dish was, he liked nothing better than pukeworm in a sesame bun with lashings of tomato and goldfish sauce.

If pukeworms were the king's favourite food then Queen Anaglypta's favourite was The Pudding That Dare Not Speak Its Name. This was a pudding so wonderful and so addictive that one quick sniff of its sickly aroma, from even fifteen rooms away, led to instant addiction for which there was absolutely no cure. Once you had tasted The Pudding That Dare Not Speak Its Name you were hooked for life and had to eat it every day.

To cook such a pudding required a very special chef. Just to read half the list of ingredients was enough to send anyone into a dribbling chocolate fantasy. To read the whole list was enough to make even the skinniest person put on fifty kilos. In twelve different rooms – each one a mile apart – twelve cooks with their noses sealed up with concrete, both arms tied behind someone else's back, stood up to their necks in cold water and mixed up seven of the eighty-four ingredients that made up The Pudding That Dare Not Speak Its Name.

Specially trained labradors then carried the twelve bowls into the six Pre-Pre-Mixing rooms where they were stirred together. The six bowls were then carried by radio-controlled traffic wardens into the three Pre-Mixing rooms where they were mixed up into new bowls. And finally, three headless robots carried the bowls into the sealed Mixing Chambers, where a blindfolded scientist with a huge number of important letters after his name, stood behind nuclear bomb-proof glass and poured everything into one final bowl with remote-control arms. A trained chicken added a cherry to the top and Queen Anaglypta was carried in on a conveyor belt and dropped right into the middle of The Pudding That Dare Not Speak Its Name. Two hours later the intoxicated queen was carried out into the Washing-Up Chamber and hosed down by her Lady in Waiting. Interestingly, the microscopic remains of The Pudding That Dare Not Speak Its Name that the queen had overlooked or that had been unable to seep into her wrinkles, were washed out through the drains into the moat where they sank into the waiting mouth of Gravalax – the largest pukeworm that had ever lived.

To everyone, Gravalax was a legend like the Loch Ness Monster. Blurred photos existed that could have been old car tyres, except that there were no cars in the country. But Gravalax was more than a legend, she was real. She lay on her back below the castle drains swallowing everything that floated, wriggled, and dropped down through the water. Like the queen she was a hopeless Pudding That Dare Not Speak Its Name addict and on the one weekend in her life that the queen went away on holiday, taking her supply of pudding with her in a small petrol tanker, Gravalax left the water for the first time in her life.

Too fat to walk on her tiny, stunted legs, she slithered across the grass, through the weeping willows and crashed through the wall into the kitchen garden. She swallowed three greenhouses, seven under-gardeners and a small forest before slithering back into the moat where she was horribly sick. All the under-gardeners survived, though they were never quite the same again. They had awful nightmares where huge carriages turned into pumpkins that they married, and the most terrifying part of the dream was that they all lived happily ever after. Frantic parents at the ends of their tether told naughty children that if they didn't go to sleep Gravalax would come and eat them alive.

Organzola, the strongest cheese in the world, was so powerful it had to be eaten underwater. It was stronger than a sumo wrestler's armpit in a heatwave, and so deadly that the wallpaper fell off the walls of any room it was taken into, followed by the plaster. It had a half-life of thirteen million years and its ingredients and the way it was made are too disgusting to write about, though I'm sure you would like me to. Just let me say that after fifty years rotting in the stomach of a pickled hippopotamus, it was only half cooked. Creepeasy the Butler had a slice of Orgnzola between two slices of rusty corrugated iron every night before going to bed and his dreams were unbelievable.

There were other strange foods in the castle. Café Olé was another good way to avoid wasting the night sleeping. More expensive than the finest champagne it was made from the fermented brains of Spanish Bullfighters. Because of the microscopic size of these brains, Café Olé was a very rare drink and only drunk by Standhardly, the nightwatchman at the main gate of Castle Twilight, to keep him awake through his long vigil. Every Monday at sunset, Standhardly was given a thimbleful of the thick sticky drink and for seven days and nights he stayed wide awake. The side-effects were strange and quite often the nightwatchman tried to arrest trees or jumped into the moat convinced his trousers were full of hedgehogs. A fly that fell into the drinking thimble stayed awake for three years which, considering it had a normal lifespan of two days, was amazing. Standhardly himself was over two hundred years old, but then so were a lot of people around Castle Twilight.

THE STREET OF
A THOUSAND CARDIGANS

Behind the Potato Market, in The Street of a Thousand Cardigans, were the homes of the Knitting Witches. In other lands witches wove spells, but here they knitted them. If you needed a spell, you went to the shop, bought a pattern and took it to the Knitting Witches. Some weekly magazines had free patterns in but they were only for small spells like cleaning the drains or turning your neighbour's dog into a different sort of dog. But even these had to be knitted by a witch, because it was against the law for anyone else to own knitting needles. If the Spells Police found any long pointed bits of wood in your house, you could end up in jail. Pencils had been exempt from this law for many years until someone was caught knitting a pimple spell while they were pretending to write a shopping list and since then even pencils were banned. When it came to knitting the Knitting Witches had the whole thing sewn up.

Halfway down The Street of a Thousand Cardigans

was The Wool Shop. This was the centre of the whole industry, for without wool, no one could knit a thing. On shelves that reached back into the mists of time, was every type of wool you could ever imagine and wools you daren't dream about. There were fine gold twines for knitting spells to make people fall in love with you. There were invisible wools to knit spells to embarrass people. There were chicken-flavoured wools, strangling wools, time-travelling wools and tartan wools. It was like a giant internet of wool. Whatever you could imagine, no matter how disgusting or ridiculous, there was a wool for it.

The shop should have been run by a huge homely woman with an enormous bosom, warm sparkly eyes and a never ending appetite for gossip and chocolate cake, but it wasn't. It was run by a mean, pinched, angry little man called Gromwell. He hated wool. He hated witches. He hated everything except Princess Chocolate, whom he loved with all his mean crumpled-up little heart. Of course, everyone loved Princess Chocolate but Gromwell didn't know that. In fact, everyone thought that they were the only person in the whole world who loved the princess, even though she was the most beautiful woman in the world and everyone was bound to love her.

'I need seven balls of Eternal-Youth wool, three of Irresistible-Charm and one of Recurring Acne,' said Eudora, a cardigan witch from across the street.

'Twenty-three balls of My-God-Haven't-You-Got-Fat chunky cashmere,' said Faucet, another knitting witch.

'I'm all out of Irresistible-Charm,' said Gromwell and all the witches in the shop fell about laughing.

'Ain't that the truth,' said Eudora.

The witches were laughing so much that they collapsed into a great heap of aprons; wool and knitting needles, arms and legs all over the place, tears pouring down their faces and knitting patterns everywhere. If the truth were known they often bought more Irresistible-Charm wool than they needed, just to make Gromwell run out. Gromwell was used to their insults but as his father before him had said – 'Someone who hates you's money's just as good as someone who likes you's.'

'How do you know that?' Gromwell used to ask him. 'There ain't no one who likes us.'

'The bank manager does,' said his father.

It was fifteen minutes before all the witches got themselves sorted out. One by one they gathered up their shopping and staggered red-faced from the shop clutching themselves and still laughing – even when they were back in their houses sat by the fire knitting. And that's when the trouble started.

In all the confusion, everyone's shopping had got muddled up and the problem was that one type of wool looked very much like another. Only a scientist with an enormous microscope could tell the difference between Fart-Loudly-In-Public-Places wool and Speak-French-Instantly wool, though in that particular case there wasn't much difference. But if you got Declare-War-On-Everyone-You-Meet wool with Be-As-Kind-As-Kitten-To-The-Nastiest-Person-In-Your-Street wool the results could be disastrous. And they were.

For weeks the most ridiculous, embarrassing, infuriating things kept happening and it was a miracle that no one got killed. Husbands fought with wives. Girls fought with boys. Dogs fought with goldfish, and Creepeasy the Butler fought with himself and lost, which happened all the time anyway.

The spells worked like this. If you wanted to do some magic, you went to the Street of a Thousand Cardigans, chose the witch who specialised in the particular magic you wanted, paid them some money and they knitted a cardigan with the right wools. Then you gave the cardigan to the person you wanted to do the magic to and when they went out wearing it, the spell was cast.

To the outsider it might seem that there was one great flaw in this. If you didn't want any magic done to you, all you had to do was not wear cardigans. But it was against the law to say no to a present. If someone gave you a cardigan, you had to wear it or go to prison where the cardigans were made of rusty steel with lots of pointed spikes inside and were bolted onto you. This hardly ever happened because as unlikely as it may seem, everyone actually liked cardigans. While the rest of the world laughed at cardigans, in the countryside around Castle Twilight they were the national costume, loved and adored by all. The more cardigans you had, the more important you felt. You could win them in lotteries. And with the right wool they could make you rich and famous.

'Cardigans don't grow on trees,' people said, but it wasn't true, they did. A long time ago someone had got fed up paying the Knitting Witches lots of money every time they wanted some magic doing so they fooled one of them into knitting a special cardigan for a tree.

'Why's it got seven arms?' said the witch, looking at the strange pattern. 'It looks a bit like a tree.'

'Well, young Gerald is rather wooden, I suppose,' said the customer with a smile, 'but his bark is worse than his bite and he is branching out in all directions, though he's always ready to bough to any suggestions as long as they don't take him away from his roots.'

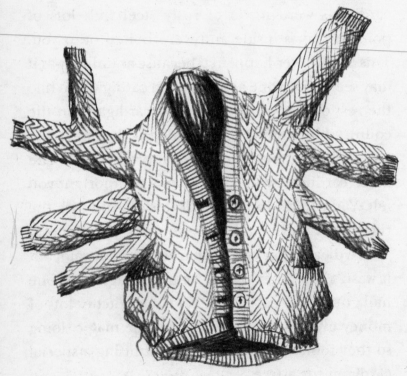

'This Gerald,' said the witch, 'result of a bad spell was he?'

'Ah, you've twigged,' said the customer. 'Well, I'll leaf you alone and come back when it's ready.'

'But you haven't said what sort of wool you want; what sort of spell you want to do,' said the witch.

'Just use up every single bit of leftover wool you've got,' said the customer.

The witch felt uneasy about the whole thing. On the other hand, with seven arms it meant she could charge a lot more and she wouldn't have to spend any money buying wool. When the cardigan was finished the customer took it out into the middle of the forest and put it on the tree.

Nothing happened. The days turned into weeks and the customer began to think she'd wasted her money. Then one night it rained, huge wild rain drops from a sky full of violent thunder and lightning. For three days and nights it rained, ditches ran like streams, streams ran like rivers and rivers ran like the wind. For three days and nights everyone stayed indoors, eating stale bread and tinned soup. Witches shouted and cursed at the clouds but nothing they did would drive them away.

On the fourth day, the sun came out. The wild water crawled back into the ground and life returned to normal. As the cock finished crowing, the customer slipped away into the forest for one last look at the tree.

There were cardigans everywhere, hundreds of them, in all shapes and sizes. Every one of them was the most beautiful garment the customer had ever seen. That night she loaded them up on her cart and took them home. Every cardigan had a thousand spells woven into it and the first spell was to forget there was a cardigan tree. Every few years someone would stumble across it in the forest, load up their cart with cardigans, try on one as soon as they got home and instantly forget where they'd got them from. A particularly honest policeman who found the tree, assumed he must have stolen the cardigans and arrested himself. There were rumours, people talked about a magic tree, but no one knew where it was.

The other spells were all out of control and muddled up. They would pop out at random, usually when the wearer was least expecting it. A young man was on his bended knee just about to ask his sweetheart to marry him when he turned into a packet of digestive biscuits. A frog kissing another frog turned into a bank manager, and a postman delivering an urgent parcel turned into a side street. No one was safe, not even the dogs and cats who slept on the cardigans. An old spaniel lifted his leg to a lamp-post as the post turned into an electric fire and it gave him a nasty shock.

'We've got to find that wretched tree,' said Eudora, 'or we'll all be out of work.'

'Maybe we could knit a cardigan that could lead us to it,' said Faucet.

'No, it's too clever for that,' said Eudora.

'Maybe we could organise search parties,' said Faucet.

'There's twenty-seven thousand million trees in the forest,' said Eudora. 'No, there's only one thing to do, we'll have to chop them all down.'

'That's against the law,' said Faucet. 'Maybe Meddler and Leaky could find it.'

'They won't help, they're on commission. They get five percent of every cheap cardigan sold,' said Eudora.

'Oh, well,' said Faucet, 'there's only one thing to do.'

'What's that?' said Eudora.

'Join a government re-training scheme,' said Faucet. 'It's time to hang up the old knitting needles. I think I'll be a hairdresser.'

At first everyone was in a terrible state. A cardigan was more than a horrible garment with lumpy pockets and leather elbow patches, it was a part of everyday life. It was a part of your soul.

'And what will we wear to keep warm?' they asked.

'How about a nice raincoat?' said Gromwell, who saw an opportunity when it presented itself.

'Raincoats? We can't have raincoats as the national costume,' said Queen Anaglypta.

'Why not, my dear,' said King Marmite. 'The British do. I think they're nice.'

'Well, at least we won't have to wear those dreadful cardigans any more,' said the queen.

Eudora wanted to fight on. She was too old to change and besides, her mother had been a Knitting Witch and so had her grandmother. She could be seen on moonlit nights creeping round the forest with a box of matches and a packet of firelighters, but every time she went out, Meddler and Leaky made it rain and all she ever burnt were her fingers.

'Maybe we could drop buckets of weed killer over the forest from balloons,' she said, but no one was listening.

'Hairdressing,' she said. 'What sort of job's that for a witch?'

But the others had already set up a salon in Gromwell's old shop and were making a fortune weaving Magic Wigs for the bald and vain.

CREEPEASY THE BUTLER

Creepeasy lived in the shadows. His skin was paler than white, and practically transparent, like frosted glass. And where it stretched tight over his knuckles and cheeks you could see his brittle old bones criss-crossed with a cobweb of veins.

'Next to a corpse,' he used to say with a cackle like breaking sticks, 'I'm very handsome.'

'Next to a corpse,' said everyone else, 'you'd be impossible to recognise.'

The corpses complained, and Creepeasy felt flattered. No one ever troubled him, no one dared. They had seen what he had done to people who did, seen him turn smart handsome clever princes into incontinent goldfish and fearless soldiers into damp puppies.

Creepeasy lived in the black cellars far below the castle, below the dungeons where the evil Baron Nauseous was imprisoned. Under the wine cellars, descending level after level was an endless network of cells and cellars where even the memory of sunshine had long ago been forgotten. Creepeasy lived in an uncharted tangle of winding dark tunnels that led from room to room, through gloomy caves the size of mansions and lit by an eerie luminous glow that revealed black bottomless lakes. The lakes reached so far down into the earth that their waters were warmed by the fury at the earth's core. Here Creepeasy lived, with alien beings, dark forces and a talking slug named Beryl.

In the darkest most secret corners of the farthest caves the enchanting and elusive Moon Mushroom grew. It was a strange white fungus with a disturbing shape and weird magical properties that changed with the phases of the moon. King Marmite was seriously addicted to the Moon Mushroom and only Creepeasy knew where it grew.

Unlike the fictitious mushroom in *Alice in Wonderland*, which actually made people change size, the Moon Mushroom just made them think they had changed size when in fact they hadn't. Grown men had been known to force themselves into jam jars whilst under its influence, and small boys vanished into large trousers, never to be seen again.

It had no real effect unless it was boiled with carrots when it really did make people change size, but only in certain and unpredictable places. Fortunately or not, depending on where it did this, the effect was only temporary, never lasting more than ten years.

When the moon was on the wane, and a black cockerel had been seen dancing on one leg on the East Tower, the effects of the mushroom could be disastrous. One cautious nibble was enough to turn them suddenly into accountants, for which there was no known cure.

'Your majesty is my only reason for living,' said Creepeasy to King Marmite in a voice that sounded like rancid butter. The king, who needed all the flattery he could get, believed him. But no one else did.

'Oh good and faithful servant,' said the king. 'Have another knighthood.'

'Your supreme-wonderful-brilliant-genius-handsome-excellency is so kind,' smarmed Creepeasy. 'It's more than I deserve, for beside you I am but a humble worm.'

'Beside a humble worm, you're but a humble worm,' muttered the queen.

'How can you say such a thing, my beloved,' said the king. 'Creepeasy is the most devoted servant we have.'

'Yes, the most devoted to himself,' she replied.

'Oh, your beautiful-adorable-wonderful-queenliness,' grovelled Creepeasy. 'You do me wrong. I would lay down my life for the king.'

'Go on then,' said Princess Chocolate.

'Who'd notice the difference?' said the queen.

'Well at least he'd be a bit quieter,' said the princess.

'I say mummy,' said Prince Bert, 'can't you just make him leave the room? He's making my caramel pudding grow mould.'

Creepeasy hated the royal family with a hatred beyond words. He lay in his bed at night and thought of disgusting ways to kill them. The king was no problem, he was an idiot. If it wasn't for the rest of them, he'd do anything Creepeasy wanted. He thought of poisoning them but since he was one of the three Royal Food Tasters, it didn't seem like a very good idea.

'Maybe I could start a revolution,' he thought. 'Get the people to rise up and storm the castle. I'd be a hero and become a king.'

The trouble was that everyone adored the royal family and everyone, except Mavis The Tadpole Lady, hated Creepeasy. It was a small country and everyone knew the king and queen personally. Who would want to overthrow a king who came to your house on your birthday and gave you a box of fudge, or a queen who, without a thought, would give you the crusts off her toast?

And of course, as everyone knew, there was no way you could do magic to kings and queens, it just bounced off them. Princes and princesses were the same. This was a blessing for the royal family but a constant source of anger to the butler. He had tried slipping spells past them, hiding them in boxes of chocolates or bunches of flowers, but all that happened was he got boils. Eventually, it had got so bad that he looked as if someone had poured a bucket of lumpy custard over him. Creepeasy was a big-time loser who, like the king, had only got his job because his father had had it before him.

'Oh Angela,' he said to his pet spider as he lay curled up in the damp green sheets of his bed, 'life is so unfair.

Angela said nothing. Spiders can't speak and it was a good job, because she hated Creepeasy as much as everyone else did. She should have been out in the vegetable garden lurking in the cabbages waiting to give people fatal bites. She should have been producing a race of toxic babies but instead she spent most of her life in a slimy jam jar in a slimy cellar miles from everything she knew and loved. She couldn't even kill Creepeasy. She bit him, she bit him over and over again, but all that happened was she got diarrhoea and the old butler got nothing.

Unfair, unfair, I'll say it is, she thought to herself.

'There must be something I can do,' said Creepeasy to Mavis The Tadpole Lady. 'Everyone hates me.'

'Well, there you are,' said Mavis. 'Every cloud has a silver lining.'

'What are you talking about?' said Creepeasy.

'How many people can say that EVERYONE hates them?' said Mavis.

'I see what you mean,' said Creepeasy, cheering up.

'You're probably the only person in the whole country that no one likes,' said Mavis. 'No one except me that is.'

She blushed and looked at her feet. She had known for years that the old butler was in love with her. Not many people can fall in love with someone with green skin who catches flies with her tongue. Creepeasy was an exception. He adored Mavis, he worshipped the ground she dribbled on but she had never told him how she felt about him before. She had always pretended she couldn't stand him, when in fact she had loved him since they were children. But for a humble tadpole lady to marry a butler was unthinkable, even a butler as vile as Creepeasy. She couldn't put her finger on what it was she loved about him. It certainly wasn't the terrible wart on his nose, or the fact you could read a newspaper through his skin. And it wasn't the wonderful shade of brown of his teeth or the click-clack his knees made when he walked. But there was something sad and endearing about him.

Everyone else looked at him with disgust; looked at him in the same way that they looked at the carpet after the dog had thrown up its dinner on it. But Mavis saw beyond that, she saw deep into his soul and saw that underneath his evil exterior, hidden deep in his nasty twisted interior, there was a faint spark of something she couldn't actually put her finger on. Actually, it was indigestion but Mavis didn't realise.

Creepeasy had loved Mavis for years, ever since he had been a spindly little boy and she had been a big fat child. From the first day he'd seen her, when she'd spat on him as he walked under an apple tree, he had worshipped the ground she had dribbled on. He had never told a soul not even Angela. He had carried a dream in his heart, in the very tiny place he kept for nice thoughts, a dream that one day she would be his, all eighty-seven kilos of her.

'I . . . er . . .' he muttered.

'Er . . . I . . .' he muttered a week later.

'Er . . . I don't suppose . . .' he blurted out a month after that.

'Um . . . er . . . well . . . er . . . I don't suppose . . . no of course you wouldn't . . .' he said finally after six months.'

'I wouldn't what?' said Mavis.

'No, of course you wouldn't,' said Creepeasy.

'Wouldn't what?'

'Wouldn't want to go to the pictures one night?' said Creepeasy. His white skin burst into scarlet as all the blood in his body rushed up to his face. He ran into the corner and put a paper bag over his head.

'Oᴋ,' said Mavis.

'What?' said Creepeasy from inside his paper bag.

'I said Oᴋ.' Mavis was blushing too by then – her green skin had gone a peculiar, brown colour.

So they went up to Mavis's tower on the roof and she cooked kidneys in slime for Creepeasy. And after dinner they sat by the fire and the old butler told her how much everyone hated him and Mavis showed him her seventy-three albums of photos of Andrew The Giant Tadpole.

'And here he is looking cross because I'd just eaten a big fly that had landed in his tank,' said Mavis.

'Mmm,' said Creepeasy.

'And here's one of him looking cheeky,' said Mavis.

'How can you tell the difference?' said Creepeasy, with a yawn. 'You haven't got any really good poison recipes, have you?'

'Silly boy,' said Mavis. 'Here, I bought you a present.'

It was a cardigan. Creepeasy felt uneasy. He adored Mavis and he felt she quite liked him too and he knew it was illegal to turn down the gift of a cardigan, but you could never tell what spells were knitted into them. He had a horrible feeling he might turn into a giant tadpole.

'Er . . .' he began.

'It's alright,' said Mavis. 'It's quite harmless.'

'Alright,' said Creepeasy, slipping his arms into the sleeves. 'Are you sure you haven't got any poison recipe—'

He never finished the sentence. As soon as the cardigan had settled round his shoulders he forgot all about poison. His eyes filled with misty tears and through the mist he saw the most beautiful woman in the world, Mavis.

'Has anyone ever told you, you look like Marilyn Monroe?' he said, grasping Mavis's hand and staring deep into her eyes. And then he started to sing. It was like the sound of someone strangling a ferret.

I love you more than castor oil,
  More than a bucket of fish,
I love you more than a gumboil,
  More than a frog that goes squish.

Your skin is as smooth as the seat of my bike,
  Your hair is like dead grass on fire,
Your eyes, either side of your nose, are just like,
  Two delicate rolls of barbed wire.

When you breathe you strip paint,
  When you dance you crack floors,

When you kiss me I faint,
  And sweat blood from my pores.

Mavis was beginning to wonder if the cardigan had been such a good idea. Creepeasy droned on for an hour before she could get it off him. Her tape-recorder had tried to commit suicide three times but it had served its purpose.

'If anyone hears about this I'll be finished,' said Creepeasy. 'My reputation will be ruined.'

'Now, now, dear,' said Mavis. 'Don't you worry yourself about that. No wife would ever betray her husband like that.'

'Wife?' said Creepeasy.

'That's right, dear,' said Mavis.

'Does the word "blackmail" mean anything to you?' said Creepeasy.

'No, not a thing,' said Mavis.

Creepeasy sighed. His admiration for Mavis was complete. At last he had met someone who was meaner and more devious than he was. What more could he want? He put his new cardigan back on and the two lovers walked off into the sunset.

THE WHINE CELLAR

At the highest point of Castle Twilight, where for days on end the towers are hidden in cloud, are the remains of the famous Prince Otto's Whine Cellar.

Prince Otto had a terrible fear of depths and built everything as far above the ground as possible. On long summer evenings he would clamber up the endless stone steps to his beloved whine cellar and spend many happy hours whining softly to himself.

The room below was the dynamite store where the explosives used for cracking extra hard walnuts were kept and in the room below that lived a solitary hermit whose only joy in life was playing with matches.

One fateful Thursday in the early November of 1757, Prince Otto lay curled up on the floor of his cellar dribbling softly into a cushion after an unusually energetic whine. The air was dry and the dynamite store full to overflowing. In his room the hermit struggled in the twilight with a jumbo match. Suddenly it ignited, throwing him across the room. A gust of wind carried the flames up the winding stairs and through the open door of the room above.

Deep down in the deepest darkest drains lazy rats heard the explosion as Prince Otto's fear of depths was finally cured forever. Three days later the feathers from his cushion slowly floated to earth like a tiny snow storm, but of the mad prince no trace was ever found.

Amazingly the hermit survived. In a shower of several million broken walnuts he was thrown down the stairs, floor after floor, until he reached the kitchens. He spent the rest of his life seven inches shorter sitting in a bucket of cold water.

The cellar was never rebuilt.

ANDREW THE GIANT TADPOLE

In the midst of the rolling acres of grey lead roof on top of Castle Twilight, shrouded in rancid green steam, stood the Place of Slime; a terrifying thing to see and even worse to smell. Inside its walls stood a gigantic tank of slime. Larger than a football field and deeper than ten double-decker buses, it was the home of Andrew The Giant Tadpole.

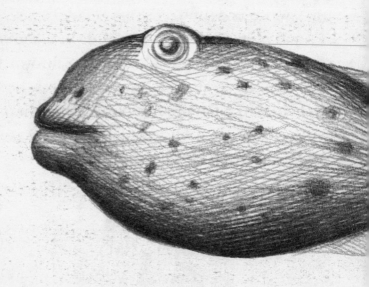

The water was thick with the green slime of centuries of decay. It hung heavy like a dense fog, and through it swam the shadowy form of the solitary black creature that could swallow a whale in one mouthful. His piggy eyes looked out with an evil glare that struck terror into the pilots of passing planes. Rumours and legends sprung up of a mysterious tadpole triangle where planes and airships were supposed to have vanished without trace. There may have been some truth in these stories for every year the tadpole grew larger and larger.

In the Middle Ages enemies of the king were brought here and cast down into the slime. As they tried to stay afloat; tried to find something to grab hold of that would save them, Andrew ate their clothes and sucked out every single hair from their bodies.

Pink, naked, and quivering like enormous jelly babies, the victims were hauled out, rolled in egg yolk and chocolate sprinkles and put back into the slime so Andrew could have dessert. Each wearing nothing but a brown paper bag, the victims were then hauled out again and made to stand in front of the king and queen.

After a session in the slime with Andrew even the fiercest and most black-hearted enemies became meek and mild. They no longer said much and frequently took up dribbling as a hobby. Only the very strange Count Floretta of Delft kept coming back for more.

Everyone lived in fear of the day when Andrew The Giant Tadpole would become Andrew The Giant Frog. But in the six hundred years since he had hatched from a mysterious frog spawn, which fell to earth one night during a strange electric storm, he didn't show the slightest hint of a bump on his body to indicate he was about to grow legs.

The post of Giant Tadpole Keeper was held by a little old lady called Mavis, descended from a long line of hereditary tadpole keepers. Mavis was actually not a little old lady, she was a huge fat old lady. Over the centuries Mavis's ancestors had grown to look like Andrew. At night she slept on an old leather water bed filled with warm slime from her beloved Andrew's tank.

And in his tank, Andrew The Giant Tadpole swam slowly around, thinking his thoughts and brooding. No one had ever heard him make a sound. Most people thought of him as no more than a large moving vegetable and no cleverer than a brussels sprout. But Andrew had telepathic powers and for the past five hundred years had been arguing with Gravalax the giant Pukeworm.

'You're no more than a large moving vegetable,' said Gravalax inside her head.

'Well if I'm a vegetable, you're just a dirty old rolled up carpet,' said Andrew inside his.

'One day, I'm going to come up there and teach

you a lesson,' said Gravalax.

'Oh yeah,' sneered Andrew. 'If pigs could fly. And if pigs could fly, it would take five hundred of them to lift a disgusting old bag like you off the ground, never mind get you up onto the roof.'

'I can do telekinesis,' said Gravalax. 'I can transport myself anywhere I want just by thinking, big fat frog's baby.'

'Thinking, thinking, you wouldn't know what thinking was if you swallowed it,' said Andrew.

'Gasbag,' said Gravalax.

'One day I'm going to come down there and teach you a lesson,' said Andrew.

'Oh, go swallow your slime,' said Gravalax.

For five hundred years these ridiculous telepathic conversations had been going on and
Andrew was getting angry. What nobody knew
was that anger was the trigger that would make
Andrew change into a frog. Ordinary tadpoles just
keep growing bumps and legs and in a few weeks
jump out of their ponds. But Andrew wasn't an
ordinary tadpole, he needed to be *really* angry to
grow legs, otherwise what was the point of all that
effort. And Andrew was getting angry.

'I'm sure that thing's changing shape,' said Creepeasy the Butler as he walked arm in arm with Mavis on the roof one late summer evening.

'I've a horrible feeling, you're right,' said Mavis.

'Do you think we should tell the king?' said Creepeasy.

'No, not yet,' said Mavis. 'It could be years before there's anything to worry about.'

But she was wrong there.

'You're the ugliest thing in the whole universe,' said Gravalax. 'Not a single hair on your whole body, it's disgusting.'

'You're, you're . . .' said Andrew. He was so angry that he couldn't think of words. He had six bumps and they were getting bigger and bigger. All he could think was, *I must have been bitten by the biggest underwater mosquito that's ever existed and it HURTS!*

'Lost your tongue, fatty?' said Gravalax. 'Got so fat, you can't open your big fat mouth?'

Andrew said nothing. The bumps had smaller bumps at the end of them and they had claws on them.

'Wow,' he thought. 'Eat your heart out Charles Darwin.'

'Fatty, fatty, blobfish,' said Gravalax.

Andrew merely smiled to himself, as only a sixty-foot-long frog can.

'Boy, are you going to wish you hadn't said that,' he said, and stood up on his four back legs. The Place of Slime had only one door. It was a big door, big enough for a Mavis to get through, but nowhere near big enough for an Andrew. He burst the glass walls of his tank, burst the stone walls of the room and set off across the castle roof, as the slime spread out around him. Creepeasy and Mavis were cuddling behind a chimney when the smell hit them.

'Are you wearing aftershave?' said Mavis.

'No,' said the butler, finding it hard not to be sick.

'Well, where's that wonderful smell coming from?' said Mavis. And then the slime ran round their ankles and Creepeasy fainted into her arms.

Andrew reached the edge of the roof and looked down into the moat. It was a long way down.

'I can see you, scumbag,' he said, and the water below him shook. The slime had covered the whole roof and was running down the castle walls. As it reached the moat, the water tried to retreat but the slime slipped into it and turned it green. The smell was terrible, or wonderful, depending on who you were.

'Can you taste me, carpetface?' said Andrew. 'Get ready to die.' And he threw himself over the edge.

Everybody who was out of doors was caught in the splash. Green sticky rain poured down on them covering everything. The moat was empty apart from puddles in the mud full of wriggling creatures trying to hide. Gravalax was too big to hide. At first she thought the end of the world had come. Everything had suddenly gone dark. The sun had vanished and the sky had fallen on top of her, except it wasn't the sky, it was Andrew. She slithered out and the two old enemies stood facing each other.

'Andrew?' said Gravalax.

'Gravalax,' said Andrew.

'You're not at all how I imagined you'd be,' said Gravalax.

'Neither are you,' said Andrew.

'I would even go so far as to say that you're quite nice looking,' said Gravalax.

'*I* would even go so far as to say that you're beautiful,' said Andrew.

'*I* would even go so far as to say that you're drop dead gorgeous,' said Gravalax.

This went on for several hours, with the two of them saying more and more flattering things about each other. People peered out from behind trees as the two hideous creatures stood facing each other. No one could hear what Andrew and Gravalax were saying because they were doing it inside their heads. To everyone else it looked as if they were staring each other down and were about to launch into the most terrible fight. But in fact, they were falling deeply in love.

'Will you marry me?' said Andrew.

'It's impossible,' said Gravalax. 'You are so far above me.'

'I was only on the roof,' said Andrew. 'Come on, give us a kiss.'

Now everyone knows what happens when you kiss a frog, it turns into a prince. So it was with Andrew. When Gravalax kissed Andrew he turned into the most beautiful prince anyone had ever seen, even more good-looking than Prince Bert. But no one, not even Gravalax, knew what happens when you kiss a pukeworm. There was a flash of light and a puff of smoke, of course, and there in front of Prince Andrew was a golden-haired labrador puppy.

'Oh, well,' said Prince Andrew. 'At least she'll love me for ever.'

PRINCE BERT

Prince Bert was like good custard; thick and beautiful. He floated through life in a happy world of his own. Outside it could be raining cats, dogs and fish but inside his head it was always sunshine. He was surrounded by a circle of magic that protected him from disasters, which would normally have killed anyone as dreamy as he was. He was also protected by Bertha the Frog.

Prince Bert began each day in the same way. At seven o'clock he got up, got dressed and followed Bertha through the castle to the dining room for that day. On Mondays they went to the Monday Dining Room. On Tuesdays they went to the Tuesday Dining Room and so on. There were also dining rooms for special days, like Christmas, and February the twenty-ninth. Without Bertha to show him the way, Prince Bert was lost. One day, when she was off laying spawn in the moat, he ended up in the broom cupboard, chewing the bristles on a ceiling brush. Prince Bert wasn't bothered, nothing bothered him. All he said when someone finally found him was that he thought breakfast was a bit chewy that morning.

'Not that I mind,' he said. 'It had an unusual flavour. A bit like I imagine a broom would probably taste.'

All in all, Prince Bert was a typical prince, except that he was beautiful, had one whole chin of his own and ears that didn't stick out like two car doors. Bertha, on the other hand, was not a typical frog. For a start, she was a lot cleverer than Prince Bert, who couldn't even catch flies with his tongue, and she could talk to him. It wasn't surprising because she had been bred especially to look after him. Her mother had looked after King Marmite when he had been a child and her daughter would probably look after Prince Bert's son when he was born.

Mind you, she thought to herself, *who on earth would fall in love with him, poor darling? I suppose Artery the Wizard will have to conjure him up a princess out of a chicken like he did for his father.*

Prince Bert had walked into a painting of a field full of sheep and was standing pressed up against the wall with his legs still going up and down.

'Hello sheep, hello trees,' he said.

'No, we're not going to look at the sheep yet,' said Bertha. 'We haven't had our breakfast.'

'Can the sheep come and have breakfast?' asked Prince Bert.

'No, dear,' said Bertha and pulled at his shoe-laces until he turned round and walked after her. What with walking into paintings and cupboards, it was usually lunchtime by the time they got down to the dining room.

So, the prince had lunch for breakfast, dinner for lunch and a big bar of chocolate before he went to bed to make up for missing his breakfast, except that he'd had lunch for breakfast. And in between he had cake, because wherever he went through the town everyone thought he looked as if he wasn't getting enough to eat and gave him cake. Sometimes it could take all afternoon to get down one street.

'I just don't know where the days go to,' said Bertha from inside Prince Bert's pocket as he walked back across the drawbridge for afternoon tea at seven o'clock one evening.

'Have you lost some then?' said Prince Bert.

'No, no. I mean, oh never mind,' said Bertha.

'You've been putting toffees in here again haven't you?'

'I'm so happy,' said Prince Bert for no apparent reason. 'I could dance.'

'I'd like to get out of your pocket first, if you're going to do that,' said Bertha.

'Come on then,' said Prince Bert. 'Out you hop.'

'I can't,' said Bertha. 'I'm stuck.'

'You can't get stuck in a pocket,' said Prince Bert.

'It's the toffee,' said Bertha.

'Well, we'll go upstairs and I'll change my trousers and then I can turn the pocket inside out, and then I can put some warm water in the sink and wash you until the toffee melts, and then you won't be stuck any more and I can dry you with a nice fluffy towel,' said Prince Bert.

'Clever boy,' said Bertha. She had never heard the prince speak such a long sentence and make sense.

'Right, OK ... er ... er ... where's upstairs?' he said.

Eventually, after a lot of trial and error, a lot of 'Hello sheep, hello trees', a lot of crashing about in cupboards, Prince Bert found his bedroom, or rather he found someone who knew where his bedroom was.

'I wonder what happened to Bertha?' he said as he got ready for bed.

'I'm still in your trousers, stupid,' shouted the frog.

'Oh, yes. Toffee,' said Prince Bert.

He turned his pocket inside out and rinsed the sticky frog under the tap.

'That looks like caramel toffee,' he said. 'My

favourite.'

And he picked Bertha up and licked her. There was a big flash of blue light and sitting in the sink where Bertha had been was a beautiful princess.

'Stop licking my knee, you idiot,' she said.

'What have you done with my frog?' said Prince Bert.

'I think it's time we had a serious talk,' said the princess.

She sat Prince Bert down on the end of his bed and explained about falling in love and how normal people preferred beautiful princesses to frogs. Then Queen Anaglypta had a chat with him and told him that nice boys didn't lick frogs, they married princesses and lived happily ever after.

Then, as the evening sun sank over the beautiful valley, the queen and Princess Bertha sat on the balcony catching flies and Prince Bert ate his chocolate and said goodnight to the sheep and the trees.

THE DEVIL IN DISGUISE

In the narrow darkness beyond the moat, between the weeping willows and the mountain, was a large walled garden. This was the kitchen garden where all the food for the castle that didn't swim or breathe was grown. It was a mysterious place where men in brown sackcloth dug and poked and forced the earth to give up its secrets, a place where carrots tied themselves in knots trying to escape and onions not only made your eyes water but gave you bruises as well.

The Gardeners were a strange secret society that even Artery the Wizard kept away from. On moonlit nights they performed ancient ceremonies in the cabbage patch – chanting and wailing and pouring mysterious liquids onto the tortured earth. By the morning, cabbages the size of cauliflowers tore themselves up by the roots and gathered in silent groups by the gate until the junior cabbage cooks came to collect them. Sometimes a rogue cabbage, helped by rebel turnips, threw itself into the moat and drowned. Sometimes the grapevines strangled themselves but mostly the vegetables grew quietly to enormous sizes and the garden was a calm and peaceful place.

'I'm bored with potatoes,' said Sickle, a cross-eyed undergardener who always kept one eye on who he was talking to and one on magnetic north. 'I want to grow raspberries or mangoes.'

'Don't be ridiculous,' said his mother. 'You have to be at least twenty years older than you are. Look at your father. Why he's only just been promoted to radishes and he's fifty.'

'But potatoes are so boring,' said Sickle in a hushed voice. He was standing with his mother at the entrance to the barrel they called home, where anyone could have heard him.

'You'll get yourself turned into gherkin if you keep talking like that,' said his mother.

But Sickle wasn't the only one who was discontented. All his friends felt the same. They were young and ambitious and had no time for the old ways. All they saw when they looked at a radish was a small red vegetable. They couldn't feel the history or tradition in growing salad for a king who was frightened of spiders.

'It's time we stood up for ourselves,' said Sickle,

as they huddled together over mugs of nettle beer in a deserted potting shed. 'It's time we gave up vegetables and moved on to something more exciting.'

'What, like plums?' said Trowel, another under-gardener.

'No, no,' said Sickle, 'something alive and dangerous.'

'What, like rhubarb?' said Trowel.

'No, no, no, forget the wretched fruit,' said Sickle.

A nervous murmur ran round the room. To talk about fruit in such a bad way was enough to get you turned into a postage stamp on a parcel to Outer Mongolia on a wet Thursday afternoon. Everyone felt frightened, but Sickle talked and persuaded and threatened until they all agreed to meet again at midnight on the next full moon.

'And can we conjure up plums then?' said Trowel.

'You just wait and see,' said Sickle. 'We'll conjure up more than fruit; even more than giant pumpkins.

In the following weeks Sickle collected all the

things he needed. He went to the library and got *Teach Yourself Witchcraft* and *How To Raise The Dead Using Everyday Household Objects*. He painted his sackcloth black and made himself a wand out of a raspberry cane. He tried to get some chicken's blood and a deadman's skull but none of the shops in the town would sell them to him without a letter from his mum.

At last, the day of the full moon arrived, and the six rebel undergardeners gathered in the old potting shed. Sickle had spent all afternoon vacuuming and dusting and drawing white circles and witchy looking symbols on the floor and Trowel had brought a bag of plums.

'In case we get hungry, or whatever we reincarnate feels lonely,' he said.

'Look, mate. Once and for all will you forget the fruit,' said Sickle, 'or we'll do nasty magic on you.'

Chanting strange low noises to himself Sickle stood in the middle of the room and began taking mysterious magical things out of a bag. He placed them one by one round the edge of the circle and then stood with his friends in a larger circle round the outside of them.

'What's that?' said Trowel, pointing at a bottle of red stuff.

'Bat's blood,' said Sickle.

'It looks like tomato sauce,' said Trowel.

'Have you got any idea how much bat's blood costs?' said Sickle. 'Come on, be reasonable. We get paid two turnips a week. How on earth can I buy bat's blood? It's ten pence a gallon.'

'And what are those things in the jam jar?' said Trowel's brother, Compost.

'Sheep's eyes,' said Sickle.

'They look like boiled sweets,' said Compost.

'OK, OK,' snapped Sickle. 'It's not my fault if this town has useless shops.'

'And what are those shrivelled up pink things supposed to be?' said Trowel.

'Look,' said Sickle, 'can we just get on. It'll be midnight soon and we'll be too late.'

Sickle opened *How To Raise The Dead Using Everyday Household Objects* and began moaning and swaying about. As the full moon rose over the mountains, he waved his raspberry cane in the air and howled.

'What are you actually doing?' said Compost.

'Summoning the Devil,' said Sickle.

'The Devil?' said Compost. 'What for?'

'Er ... er ... well,' said Sickle. 'Look, stop interrupting. I can't concentrate.'

'Won't he be angry,' said Compost, 'being dragged out of bed in the middle of the night?'

'Who?' said Sickle.

'The Devil.'

'Don't be stupid,' snapped Sickle. 'The Devil doesn't go to bed.'

He hadn't thought about what would happen if they did actually make the Devil appear. It had just seemed like a good idea at the time. He stopped swaying and started picking his nose. The others looked at their feet or their watches and muttered about how late it was, and wasn't it time they all went to bed.

'It won't work anyway,' said Compost. 'Not without real blood and stuff.'

All the time this had been going on, Trowel had been sitting in the corner drinking bottle after bottle of nettle beer.

'Wait a minute,' he said, staggering to his feet, 'give me the wand. I want to have a go.'

He grabbed the wand and book from Sickle and began weaving in and out of the circle.

'Woooo arrrr,' he moaned, and the others started giggling. He tripped over the jar of boiled sweets and fell onto the jar of tomato sauce which went all over him. 'Weeee owwwww,' he went on, crawling round the room with ketchup pouring down his face.

The others were doubled up with laughter now, rolling on the floor and holding their sides. All except Sickle, who just stood there glaring at them. He was furious but no matter what he said the others ignored him.

He stood in the middle of the room shouting at them to grow up and as he did so the clock struck midnight and the moonlight poured in through the skylight right into his eyes. There was a flash of lightning, a terrible smell of burning hair and a dreadful explosion. As the smoke cleared, everyone sat up sober and silent, and there in the middle of the room, where Sickle had been standing, was a chicken.

Snatched from an afterlife as a ghost flying above the fields of Tasmania, Ethel the Chicken had returned, and she had a mean look in her eye.

'Wow,' said Compost. 'Is that the Devil?'

'I don't know,' said Trowel. 'I suppose the Devil could disguise himself as anything, being the Devil.'

'A chicken seems a bit of an understatement,' said Compost.

Ethel fluffed up her feathers, closed her eyes and laid an egg. It was the weirdest egg they'd ever seen. Dark green with bumps all over it, it looked just like a hand grenade.

'That's the weirdest egg I've ever seen,' said Compost. 'It looks just like a hand grenade.'

'No, it can't be a hand grenade,' said Trowel. 'It hasn't got a pin . . .'

The undergardeners tripped and stumbled and raced out of the potting shed. A few seconds later there was an almighty explosion and, as if by magic, the shed changed into a smoking crater.

'Where's Sickle?' said Compost.

'Where's the chicken?' said Trowel.

There was another explosion behind the frightened undergardeners and pieces of broken wheelbarrow and cow manure came raining down on them.

'Why couldn't we have got a chicken that laid golden eggs?' said Trowel.

'Don't be stupid,' said Compost. 'That sort of thing only happens in stories.'

'Oh, and I suppose a chicken laying hand grenades is what happens in real life is it?' said Trowel.

There was another explosion further off. The undergardeners hurried away in the opposite direction trying to look as if they had just been out for an innocent evening stroll, which, considering it was after midnight, was rather difficult. They ducked down between the brussels sprouts as the nightwatchman went by. There had been a lot of parsnips stolen in the past few months and Toxic, the head gardener, had ordered extra security in the vegetable garden.

'What are we going to do about the chicken?' whispered Compost.

'Keep out of its way, of course,' said Trowel.

'It's nothing to do with us,' said Trowel. 'It was Sickle, and he's disappeared.'

'Do you reckon he got blown up in the shed?' said Compost.

'Maybe he is the chicken,' said Trowel.

But they were both wrong. Sickle was in Tasmania. As the clock had struck midnight and the moon had struck him in the face, he had been transformed into a ghost. Now he was floating above Tasmania surrounded by the ghosts of seven thousand dead chickens, all of whom expected him to feed them. One by one, all seven thousand of them pecked at his shoes and when they had all had a go, they started again and again and again. Sickle was not happy.

Ethel the Chicken, on the other hand, was very happy. Up until then she had been floating over

Tasmania for fifty years and knew it like the back
of her foot and had been bored out of her mind.
Now she was back on the ground with the sweet
smell of damp earth all around her. If she could
just stop her eggs exploding everything would be
perfect. She ran across the vegetable garden to
where she could hear other chickens muttering
and clucking to each other.

There was a tall fence, taller than most chickens could fly over, and on the other side, huddled together in a hollow of damp bare earth, were a small group of scraggy chickens. The full moon shone down on them, covering them with a sad, blue glow. They were a sorry sight, feathers falling out everywhere, skinny as rats and with all the sparkle gone out of their eyes.

'Hello,' said Ethel. 'What's the matter with you?'

One of the chickens limped over to the fence and collapsed against the wire. Up close she looked even worse. Her legs were scratched and swollen. Her eyes were weeping and her wings hung down like broken sails.

'We're starving,' she said. 'We're too old to lay eggs, so they don't feed us any more. We are Brenda the Soup Chickens.'

'That's terrible,' said Ethel. 'Can't you escape?'

'Look at the fence,' said Brenda. 'If we were young and healthy we might be able to fly away, but not now.'

The other Brenda shuffled over and collapsed in a heap. Ethel's heart felt heavy and angry.

'There are only seven of us left,' said Brenda One. 'Last week there were eight. Next week one more of us will be in the soup pan. It won't be long and then it will all be over.'

'Not if I've got anything to do with it, it won't,' said Ethel. 'I have a plan. I'm going to rescue you.'

'Oh, don't bother,' said Brenda Two. 'You'll just get into trouble and end up in the soup too.'

'Don't you want to escape?' said Ethel.

'Not really,' said Brenda Four. 'This is our destiny.'

Ethel walked along the fence until she was a safe distance from the Brendas and laid an egg. She ran clear and ten seconds later it exploded, blowing a hole in the fence.

'Come on,' she said, 'run for it.'

'Run, run?' said Brenda One. 'We can't run.'

'Run for what?' said Brenda Two.

'Well, limp for it,' said Ethel, 'but get a move on.'

The seven old chickens hobbled and collapsed and shuffled and hobbled some more, until they were all through the hole in the fence.

'Come on,' said Ethel. 'We've got to get away before daylight.'

'I can't go on,' said Brenda Five. 'Leave me and save yourselves.'

'Don't be pathetic,' said Ethel. 'This isn't a war movie. This is real life. Come on.'

For the next three hours Ethel shoved and threatened and coaxed the Brendas until, as the morning sun began to creep over the rooftops, they were all safely away from the castle, hidden in the bushes, half-way up the mountain. For the next six weeks they drank the clear water from the mountain stream, which, as everyone who has ever visited the valley knows, gives you eternal life. They ate magical berries and slugs the size of cucumbers until once again they were as fit and healthy and beautiful as they had been in their youth.

'Now,' said Ethel, 'it's revenge time.'

'Right on,' said Brenda One.

'Go for it,' said Brenda Two.

'Let's kick ass,' said Brenda Three, even though she didn't have the faintest idea what it meant.

'I think you mean, let's kick donkey,' said Brenda Four. 'Those are donkeys over there, not asses.'

'What are we going to do, then?' said Brenda Six.

'First of all, we'll go and rescue all the other chickens,' said Ethel. 'And then we'll teach the humans a lesson.'

That night there was no moon. The stars slept behind heavy clouds and it was as dark as coal. Ethel slipped unnoticed through the kitchen garden and blew a hole in the main chicken run. Apart from Norman the cockerel, who was too proud and stupid to be bossed around by a hen, the twenty-seven chickens slipped quietly away into the forest to where the seven Brendas were waiting.

'Now we are Ethel and The Thirty-Four Brendas,' said Brenda One.

'Could we be The Chicken Liberation Front?'

said Brenda Fourteen.

'But we're already liberated,' said Brenda Two.

'Well how about Hell's Chickens?' said Brenda Twenty-Seven.

'What about The Big Fluffy Hens?' said Brenda Thirty, who didn't quite understand the revenge thing.

'Look, it doesn't matter what we call ourselves,' said Ethel. 'Just as long as we make life as uncomfortable for the humans as they made it for you.'

'And when we're not doing the revenge stuff,' said Brenda Thirty, 'can we learn how to do knitting?'

'Look,' said Ethel. 'We're supposed to be urban guerrillas.'

'I don't want to be a gorilla,' said Brenda Thirty, 'I want to be a big fluffy hen.'

In the end it was decided that most of the chickens would stay in the woods and peck about, eating worms and laying eggs for passing hedgehogs and foxes, while Ethel and the original seven Brendas would do the revenge stuff. Brenda Four thought that perhaps she would stay behind too because the knitting sounded quite interesting, so it was Ethel and six Brendas. But then Brenda Five thought she might be coming down with a cold and didn't want to give them away with her sneezing, so it was Ethel and five Brendas who set off at midnight to wreak their revenge.

'Are we going to kill people?' said Brenda Two.

'No, of course not,' said Ethel. 'We're just going to scare them and make their lives as uncomfortable as possible.'

REWARD
FOR
THE CAPTURE
OF THE
MAD BOMB GANG
WHO PROBABLY LOOK LIKE

BOM

AND DON'T LOOK AT ALL LIKE
A BUNCH OF CHICKENS

CHICKEN
LAUGH

And that was what they did. Every night they came down from the mountain and created as much havoc as they could. Sometimes Ethel laid an egg on a giant pumpkin, just as the nightwatchman was approaching. Sometimes she slipped into the kitchens, down secret tunnels known only to chickens, and laid her egg in a basket full of real eggs. If she timed it just right she could catch one of the cooks just as they went by. She blew holes in boats just as someone set off to row across the moat. She blew holes in the pavement just before someone carrying a priceless glass vase came round the corner. She even walked right through the front door of the castle and laid an egg in the king's lavatory. And all the time no one suspected it was a chicken.

Posters went up in town offering a reward for the capture of the desperate gang of bandits that were causing explosions everywhere. And all the time Ethel and the five Brendas went undetected even by the all-seeing eyes of the witches Meddler and Leaky, who were too stupid to guess a few chickens had anything to do with it. The witches were so useless they mistook the chickens for a flock of pigeons.

'It's amazing those poor pigeons don't get killed when the explosions go off,' they said. 'The stupid birds always seem to be right near where it's happening.'

Then, for no apparent reason, whatever strange spell Esther had picked up, as she had been whisked through the air from Tasmania, began to wear off. Her eggs stopped looking like hand grenades and began to look like nice ordinary brown eggs. The trouble was that they still exploded, sometimes, which was rather embarrassing. She would creep up to something she wanted to blow up and lay an egg and it would just sit there. Other times somebody would find one of her eggs, take it home for tea, set their watch for three and a half minutes, nip out to the toilet, and the saucepan would explode. It was a miracle that no one was hurt.

Gradually Ethel's eggs returned to normal with only the occasional explosion. It was enough to stop the whole town eating eggs for a while. No one wanted to keep chickens any more. After two weeks everyone got sick of chicken soup three times a day and the rest of the hens were turned out to fend for themselves, which suited them fine. The original Brendas led them to the woods where they lived happily ever after, drinking from the stream of eternal life and eating all the slugs they wanted. On warm summer evenings the forest was full of fat contented chickens clucking quietly to themselves, while Ethel, the oldest chicken in the world, dreamt her dreams in the branches of a wide oak tree.

THE SECRET ROOMS

High above the tree line, tucked under the eaves of the castle, was a line of tiny windows that looked out like black eyes from a long corridor of secret rooms. These were The Secret Rooms which was a strange name because everyone knew about them. They were even advertised in tourist brochures, and renting them out made the king and queen a lot of money.

People came from all over the world and beyond to visit these rooms. Here, behind soundproof doors, they did whatever it was they loved to do to their hearts content without upsetting anyone. Those people who wanted to remain anonymous were given large plain brown paper bags to put over their heads. Some people only went for the paper bags.

On any one day if you were to peep into the row of rooms as you passed, you might have found one person listening to Norwegian pop music, another scratching their fingernails across a large blackboard and yet another reciting Welsh poetry. People with uncontrollable urges to cut stiff cardboard with rough knives went there. So did those whose only pleasure in life was listening to a wet hippopotamus wriggling in mud.

And at the far end of the corridor, unlit and cold, half hidden by cobwebs and secrecy, was the room where the shadowy strange people with the most disgusting habits in the world went. They were habits so horrible, so unspeakably vile, that it was almost impossible to write them down; habits that sent normal, sane people screaming out into the night and turned them into white-haired gibbering idiots. For there, in their twilight subhuman world, were the people who sucked large crisp cotton handkerchiefs. And worse still, beyond them, mad-eyed in coal-dark corners, insane dentists filled their own mouths with very dry cotton wool.

WHERE THE NIGHT
GOES ON FOREVER

Where the night goes on forever,
    And dawn is just a dream,
And everyone's so far away,
    That no one hears you scream.

When the dreams go on forever,
    And the sheets wrap round you tight,
And night has killed the light of day,
    And fantasies take flight.

And the dreams go on forever,
    Not creeping round your bed,
Not hiding in the darkness,
    But right inside your head.

THE HEROIC ROOMS

In medieval times, when there were lots of dragons everywhere and loads of beautiful princesses to be rescued, life was pretty chaotic. Princes from far-off lands charged about all over the place looking for the princesses, sometimes for weeks on end without sight or sound of a royal maiden.

To make things easier for everyone The Heroic Rooms were built and all the princesses in the land were installed in them. The dragons hung around together in the woods behind the kitchen garden roaring a lot and trying to outdo each other with their fire-breathing, while the princes tiptoed round the side of the castle to rescue the beautiful princesses.

A catalogue was printed giving details of each princess so that all the brave prince had to do was go to the right bedroom window, pay an outrageous amount of money to hire a ladder from the Keeper Of The Ladders, and climb up and rescue the princess of his choice.

Unfortunately, quite a few of the princes had

no chins and were terribly spotty, some were even called Kevin, and not surprisingly the sight of them appearing at the window made the princesses rush out and hire long sticks from the Keeper Of The De-Princing Poles with which they pushed the princes and their ladders into the moat. This usually resulted in the ladder getting broken and the prince having to forfeit his enormous deposit of gold he had given to the Keeper Of The Ladders.

The custom ended when the princes ran out of money and all the princesses ran off to the South of France with the fabulously wealthy Keeper Of The Ladders. Also, the price of firelighters went up so much that the dragons could no longer afford them and the sight of a dragon blowing damp smoke couldn't even frighten a small whippet.

The Heroic Rooms now lie vacant under a soft coat of mauve dust.

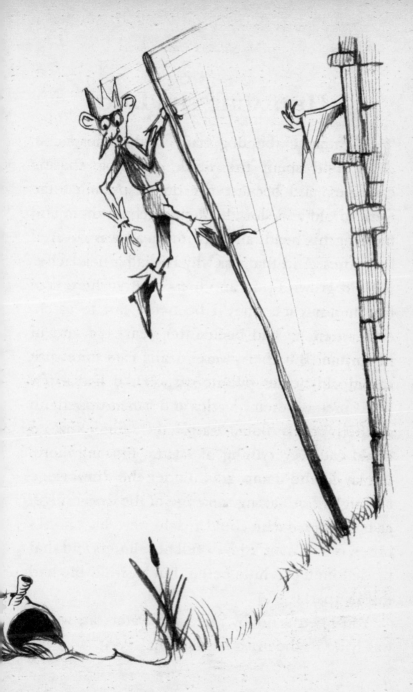

HEADACHE THE DOG

Headache the dog had another headache. He'd spent the whole morning chasing carriages, and because the horses pulling them were so old and slow, he kept catching them and banging his head, and his forehead was covered in bruises. And that was why he had a headache.

He'd grown up in another country where they had motor cars. They'd been too fast to catch, even when he had been three years old and in his prime. But there weren't any cars here, just stupid old horses pulling carts. He'd had a few policemen off their bicycles and babies tipped out of their prams, but it wasn't the same. Now he could catch everything, it was no fun any more. He lay in the damp grass under the drawbridge and sighed. All along the edge of the drawbridge, as far as Headache could reach, were big chunks bitten out. His mouth was full of splinters and that made him feel a little better, but basically life had lost its sparkle.

'You need a hobby,' said the water rat, which was lying in the grass beside him.

'Like what?' said Headache.

'I dunno,' said the water rat. 'What are you interested in?'

'Chasing cars,' said Headache.

'What's a car?' said the water rat.

'Exactly,' said Headache. 'It's all so boring.'

There was a crashing and creaking above them as a horse and carriage came out of the castle. Headache pulled himself up and ambled out onto the drawbridge.

'Oh well,' he said. 'Back to work.'

As the carriage passed him he lunged at the nearest wheel and took three spokes out in one great bite. The carriage toppled. Headache took another bite, and that was the last thing he remembered. Everything went black.

'How's my little soldier today?' said a voice like an angel.

Headache opened his eyes and looked up into the face of the most beautiful girl he had ever seen. It was Princess Chocolate and he was 'indoors'. He'd never been 'indoors' before. It was warm and the sky was very low and had cobwebs on it.

Princess Chocolate was stroking his forehead. No one had ever stroked his forehead before. No one had ever wanted to get close enough to him to do so.

'Would my little darling like a cake?' said the princess.

'Do birds fly?' thought Headache. 'Do socks smell?'

Princess Chocolate sat down beside him and fed him big forkfuls of Black Forest Gateau with cream. Headache felt something strange happening near his bottom. He looked round and his tail was wagging.

It's never done that before, he thought. *Must be something in the cake.*

He ate and ate, and then settled down to sleep on a big red velvet cushion. The princess stroked his ears and Headache floated off into his favourite dream. He was sitting in the middle of a wide, straight road and next to him was a brand new shiny Rolls Royce with fifteen princesses inside it. The car purred to life and set off down the road. When the car was at full speed, Headache slowly counted down from ten and ran after it. In fifteen seconds he caught it, the back bumper crumpled between his mighty jaws and after another fifteen seconds, the car stopped, unable to pull itself away from Headache The Mighty, with his Jaws Of Steel.

The weeks passed and Headache began to treat the castle as home. He followed Princess Chocolate everywhere with a stupid, moony expression on his face. When the princess was asleep or out, he wandered off into the darkest corners until he knew the inside of the huge building better than anyone. He visited dungeons and cellars where man had not trod for hundreds of years. Strange creatures had evolved in these dark forgotten places, creatures that Headache felt he had a lot in common with. They were ugly, they smelt awful and they scratched a lot. And in the same way that Headache worshipped Princess Chocolate, these unfortunate mistakes of nature adored Headache. He was like a magical god from a wonderful land beyond The Tunnels. He told them amazing stories of life on the other side and some of them were true.

'Up there,' he said, 'I am a king.' And all the squashy, wriggly creatures believed him.

'We didn't even know there was anywhere else except The Tunnels,' said a long worm, covered in matted wet fur.

'And my name is King Headache the Incredible,' said Headache.

'What's in a name?' asked the worm, and Headache explained.

'What, and everybody has a different one?' said the worm.

'Yes, of course they do,' said Headache. 'Don't you?'

'No,' said the worm, or it might have been a different worm, Headache wasn't sure.

'What do you call each other?' he said.

'Oi You,' said the worm.

'Or – Hey You,' said another worm.

'What do you want?' said three hundred worms and assorted slimy creatures.

'How do you know who's who?' said Headache.

'We don't,' said the worm. 'It's very difficult.'

'I think it's something to do with evolution,' said a slimy green thing. 'I don't think we get names until we develop legs.'

'Even my fleas have got names,' said Headache.

'Could we have some names?' said the worm.

'I don't see why not,' said Headache. 'Are you a boy or a girl?'

'What's that, then?' said the worm.

'Never mind,' said Headache. 'You can be called Kevin.'

'Names, evolution,' said a particularly slimy creature. 'No good'll come of it. It'll end in tears.'

'No it won't,' said Headache. 'Dogs can't cry.'

'But we can,' said the creature.

'Don't you want a name, then?' said Headache.

'No,' said the creature.

But all the others did, and the trouble was that they all wanted to be called Kevin. Headache tried to make them form a queue so he could give them each a different name, but it was a waste of time. Some worms were so enthusiastic they got in the queue twice and ended up with a different name for each end of themselves.

'Now we've got proper names and everything, oh great king,' said Kevin the Worm. 'Can we come Upstairs?'

'Will you lead us to freedom, oh great one?' said another Kevin the Worm.

Headache thought of how everyone would react to soft slimy worms the size of dolphins with sticky matted fur and a smell like nine-week-old cooked prawns.

'Why not?' he said. 'Follow me.'

All the creatures formed a line and Headache

led them through the maze of corridors towards the lower cellars. It soon became obvious though that he'd taken the wrong turning and after two hours he had to admit he was hopelessly lost.

'I'm hopelessly lost,' he said.

'I told you it would end in tears,' said Not Kevin.

'Is this Upstairs then?' said Kevin the Worm.

'It's good isn't it?' said some other Kevin the Worm.

Not Kevin began to cry and because all the creatures were pretty simple lifeforms with very little individual thought, all the others started crying too.

Pretty soon Headache was standing up to his knees in tears. The creatures, who cried quite often, were used to it and wriggled around under the water. And as it grew deeper, it started to move, slowly at first like a gentle country stream and then quicker and quicker until it was racing like a torrent. Headache began to move too. At first he managed to stay still by swimming against the current, but soon it got stronger and lack of exercise and too much Black Forest Gateau with cream had made him fat and lazy. Faster and faster he went, deeper and deeper underground, through an endless maze of winding tunnels that he'd never seen before. Side tunnels and big dark doors, steps leading up into darkness, windows looking out onto nothing all flashed by as the helpless dog was carried further and further downstream away from the castle.

On top of his head, Headache's fleas held on for all they were worth. At that moment, Headache rounded a bend and there in the distance was a speck of light. It became a circle of light and as the dog raced forward it became the end of the tunnel and he shot out in a great spout of water and landed in a puddle in the middle of a beautiful meadow of flowers.

'Oh, there you are,' said a familiar voice.

It was Princess Chocolate. She was doing what all princesses everywhere have to do every summer afternoon between just after lunch and just before tea, she was sitting in the grass in a white cotton frock making daisy-chains.

'Where have you been? You're filthy,' she said. 'It's time you had a bath.'

'Not more water,' thought the sodden dog.

'Not more water,' thought the fleas.

Princess Chocolate put a necklace of daisies around Headache's neck and led him back towards the castle.

'I wish you could talk, then you could tell me all your adventures,' she said. 'Still, I suppose all you've been doing is lying around sleeping and eating cake.'

THE PORRIDGE PAGODA

Most people think that porridge was invented in Scotland but this is not so. Porridge was actually invented, like most things, in China around 734 BC and is named after the place it was first made, a small factory on a ridge above the town of Po. The ancient Chinese, of course, were far too sensible to actually put it in their mouths. They stuck to using it for what it was intended for, namely building houses.

In 1723, a Welsh missionary managed to smuggle a consignment of porridge out of China down the legs of his trousers. The finest scientific minds of Britain were put to work, analysing the substance that the Chinese had taken for granted for centuries, and, within a mere fifteen years, had discovered that one of the main ingredients was oats. Seven years later they isolated the other ingredient, water.

The Porridge Pagoda, set high on the roof of Castle Twilight, was the first building ever constructed in the Western world from the newly synthesised porridge and, to this day, stands as fine as the day it was built. Solid proof of the durability of porridge.

Buildings sprang up everywhere. Porridge was a great success until, one night in late September 1781, a cartload of singing Scotsmen stopped at a new tavern on the outskirts of Carlisle that had just been built of porridge. Finding the innkeeper completely sold out of gruel they ate the inn. Within three weeks half of Carlisle was homeless and half of Scotland was overweight.

Nowadays of course porridge is eaten by one and all and only used for building complicated motorway flyovers and council flats.

THE ROTUNDA

The rotunda is where people who couldn't stop eating were sent. It was entirely lined with mirrors; all the walls, the ceiling and even the floor were covered with them. The overeater was stripped naked and locked in.

It was here that the greediest child in the whole history of the world was locked up with nothing to eat but a small brown loaf and a stick of celery. He survived for fifteen years by eating all the furniture, his wrist watch and seventy-nine thousand bars of milk chocolate that he had managed to smuggle in under his rolls of fat.

When the doctors came to release him he had grown up into the spottiest person in the whole history of the world and was immediately shut out of sight in a dark cellar where he lived for many years on nasty spiders and damp newspapers. He later became a famous politician.

The room was taken out of service when a chance sunbeam shone into the room and bounced around from mirror to mirror, growing in strength until it was as hot as the core of the sun. The fierce heat melted all the mirrors into a rather interesting glass blob that was later sold as a modern sculpture for three-hundred-thousand pounds.

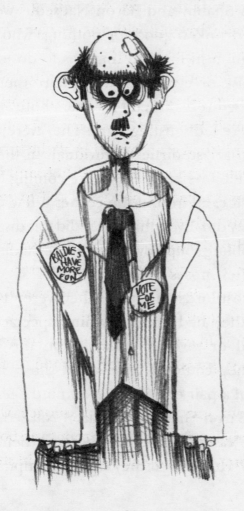

Baron Shabby
and Baron Nauseous

Baron Shabby and Baron Nauseous were two lazy drunken good for nothings who shared one ambition in life and that was to do less than anyone else or even less than each other which often proved very difficult for them both. The two barons were a disgusting sight. They were the two scruffiest, laziest, dirtiest individuals in the whole town. You always knew they were coming because their smell came round the corner a few minutes before they did. Everything they did was disgusting, from dribbling soup down their tunics at dinner, to picking their noses and eating it.

Like most lords and ladies they weren't barons because they had done anything spectacular or wonderful or saved the king from the jaws of death. They couldn't have saved the king from the jaws of a pair of pliers, never mind a ferocious dragon. Baron Shabby and Baron Nauseous were totally useless and only barons because their fathers had been. However, if they'd had Olympic Games at Castle Twilight, and if being lazy was a sport, the two barons would have won gold medals.

Because they were barons, though, they were allowed to live in the castle and the king had to feed and clothe them.

'What on earth are we going to do with them?' said King Marmite.

'It's difficult, isn't it?' said Queen Anaglypta.

'I mean, they're totally useless,' said the king.

'Maybe they could be accountants,' said the queen.

'What are they, then?'

'That's cruel,' said the king when the queen told him.

They tried putting them in charge of the lawn mowers, but within a week the grass was three feet tall and all the machines had gone rusty. They let them look after the drawbridge but in less than a fortnight woodworm, dry rot, wet rot and white ants had eaten the whole thing away.

'We need to give them something to do that doesn't need doing,' said the queen. 'That way, whatever they do, it won't spoil anything.'

'And whatever it is,' said the king. 'It needs to be done as far away from us as possible.'

'Well, the farthest away you can get from here is right down the other end of the valley, past the great forest, by the big lake on the border between here and Transylvania,' said the queen.

'Oh, you mean Transylvania Waters,' said the king.

So Baron Shabby and Baron Nauseous were sent to run the border post which was the only way into the place. They got so drunk every night that they stayed in bed until lunchtime and they got so drunk at lunchtime that they slept until night time. From a quarter to seven until seven o'clock every evening, they were sober and awake enough to stamp visitor's passports and let them through, except weekends when they were closed.

Because very few people had the patience to wait around all day and even fewer could stand the smell, the country remains unspoilt, peaceful, happy and blissfully unaware of all the terrible things going on in the rest of the world, And this is why hardly anyone has ever heard of the country beyond Transylvania where Castle Twilight hides in the mist at the end of a strange and peaceful valley.

*If you enjoyed
Castle Twilight
you'll love*

The Haunted Suitcase

THE HAUNTED SUITCASE

Under the roof of the house, below dark beams carved from the ribs of ancient sailing ships, was the attic. Hardly anyone ever went up there. It was a calm quiet place where the air stood still and the sounds from the rooms below were muffled by a heavy layer of dust. A thin wash of sunshine came in through a single skylight, throwing a million shadows around all the junk stored there. Boxes of books and old photographs, and chests full of ancient memories filled the place. In the darkest corners there were crumbling trunks that had stood there for hundreds of years. And in those time-worn containers, in soft paper-lined tunnels lived the most horrendous spiders you could imagine. They had been there so long that they had evolved into a unique species, a species that, because they had eaten nothing but books for hundreds of generations, had developed into a race of super-intelligent beings.

Because of the spiders, there were no ghosts in the attic. Even the most ferocious ghost was too frightened to live there. And even the most stupid ghost was not so stupid that he didn't shake with fear at the thought of them. All except one ghost, and it had no choice. Unable to move by any means, flight, telepathy or plain walking, it sat in the middle of the floor, terrified out of its tiny mind. It shone in the moonlight, a dull brown glow of antique leather. Nothing went near it, not even the dust. It was the haunted suitcase.

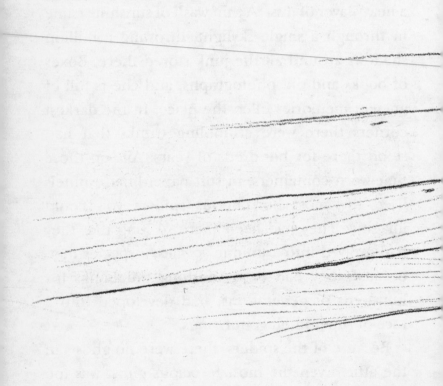

THE HAUNTED SUITCASE

It was forty years since the last person had been up into the attic. The suitcase had been there then. It gave off an uneasy feeling that made people keep away from it. Sixty years before someone had put a box of old magazines up there. The suitcase had been there then too. And in 1890, when the house-keeper had been up looking for a lost maid, the suitcase had definitely been there.

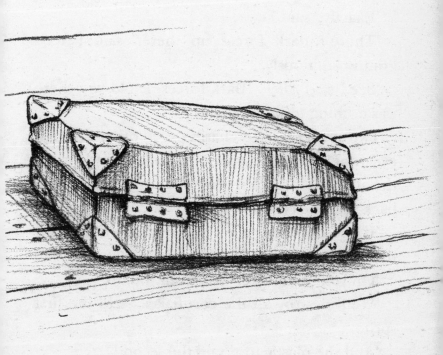

'Can we go up in the attic and play?' asked Alice one morning at breakfast.

'I suppose so,' said her mother.

'Who's *we*?' asked Peter.

'You and me,' said Alice.

'No way,' said Peter. 'I'm not going up there. It's much too dangerous.'

'Who says?' said Alice. 'I've never heard a single sound from up there.'

'Exactly,' said Peter.

'There's dark forces up there,' said Peter's granny ominously.

'See,' said Alice. 'Dark forces. I told you there was nothing to worry about.'

Two sprites started chasing each other through everyone's breakfast, splashing milk everywhere, so the attic was forgotten while they tried to get them back into the cereal box.

'If you don't let us out,' they shouted through the cardboard, 'you'll be sorry.'

'Oh yes,' said Alice. 'What will you do?'

'We'll destroy all the cornflakes,' said the first sprite.

'And the plastic toy,' said the second.

'Yeah,' said the first. 'We're cereal killers.'

By the time they'd wiped the table with the ghost of a witch's cat and finished their breakfast everyone was talking about someone else. But at lunchtime, Peter's father said, 'You know it's funny you should mention the attic. I've been thinking we should clear it out.'

'Best let sleeping dogs lie,' said Peter's granny.

'Are there dogs up there as well?' asked Alice. 'Let's go up please, please.'

'It'll end in tears,' said Peter's granny.

But after lunch they got a ladder, and Peter's father opened the trap door, climbed into the loft and disappeared.

For a long time there was complete silence. Peter and Alice stood at the bottom of the ladder looking up into the dark square in the ceiling.

'Dad,' said Alice, 'can we come up?'

'I think we should stay here and hold the ladder,' said Peter.

'You're just a big baby,' said Alice and climbed up after her father. Once again there was complete silence.

'Dad, Alice,' said Peter, 'is everything all right?'

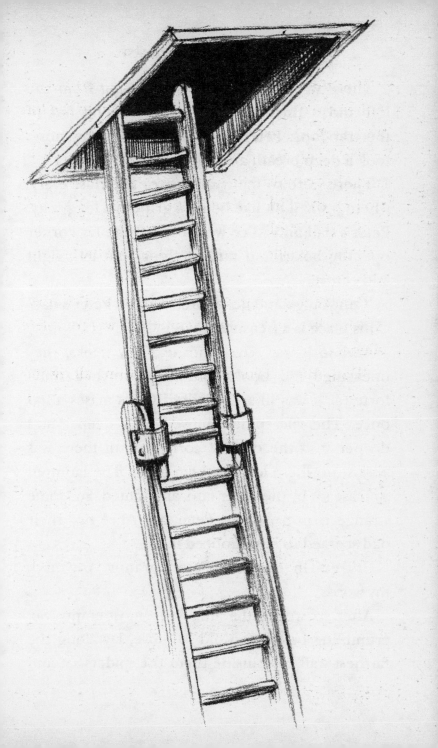

There were shuffling noises coming from the loft and a thick cloud of dust crawling out of the trapdoor. Peter put his hand over his nose, took a deep breath and climbed up the ladder.

There were so many old boxes and dust everywhere it was a bit like being a giant in a foggy city. Peter's dad and Alice were over in the far corner opening boxes and pulling things out left, right and centre.

'Can you go and get a torch?' asked Peter's dad. 'This place is a treasure trove.'

And so it was. Over the next few weeks, they unearthed old books and vases worth a small fortune. It was like a hundred Christmases all at once. The vile spiders moved back deeper and deeper into the darkest corners until there was almost nowhere left for them to go. The haunted suitcase sat by the water tank and waited. For some strange reason neither Peter nor Alice nor their dad seemed to have noticed it.

'It'll end in tears,' said Peter's granny. 'You mark my words.'

After six weeks, the attic was almost empty. Six crumbling boxes, too old to move, lay along the farthest wall, and inside them the spiders sat and waited. For the first time in three hundred years, they were frightened. It was a strange, exciting feeling but none of them knew how to handle it. Ghosts and ghouls they could deal with, but humans, especially small girls who looked like they might eat spiders, they were something different.

'Maybe we should rush out and terrorize them,' said the oldest spider, Eddie.

'Yeah,' said his sister Edna, 'If all the ghosts are scared of us, a few humans'd be easy.'

'I don't know,' said Eddie's brother, Eric. 'There are three of them.'

'Yeah,' said Eddie, 'but there are three thousand nine hundred and seventy two of us.'

'Three thousand nine hundred and seventy one,' said Edna. 'I've just eaten young Eamon.'

'I'm not sure about that girl,' said Eddie. 'She looks like she could eat all of us in one go.'

'Come on,' said Edna. 'We're the most ferocious spiders in the world.'

'Of course we are,' said Eddie. 'Let's go.'

So on the count of seven they all ran out. As they raced across the floor they suddenly heard a dreadful ear-shattering roar.

'I wonder why all spiders have names beginning with "e",' thought Edna as the roar came closer and closer. For centuries the spiders had lived in the attic. They had heard ten thousand thunderstorms and the bombs of several wars but that had all been outside. This noise was inside, right there all around them and it was the loudest thing they had ever heard.

'Oh look,' said Alice, as she vacuumed the ancient Chinese carpet that covered the attic floor,' 'hundreds of tiny weeny spiders.'

They may have frightened ghosts and they may have thought they were the most ferocious spiders in the world, but because they had lived alone for so long they had forgotten that they were also some of the smallest spiders in the world, so small that Alice could hardly see them.

'Hello, tiny spiders,' she said. 'Come and play inside the vacuum cleaner . . .'